Ley Lines

Ley Lines

The Wise Ones Book 2

Lisa Lowell

Contents

Chapter 1

The Hanging

Gailin's knees knocked together in fear as she stepped shakily up onto the gallows. You will not be frightened, she ordered herself silently. The gathered crowd of gawking villagers swam before her eyes, making her dizzy. She tried not to look at the two other men who already swung from the cross beam. One still kicked and jerked obscenely, but the clinical part of Gailin's brain knew that was because the hangman had moved the knot to the back of his neck instead of off to the side where the abrupt fall would instantly snap his neck. Instead the pathetic man must strangle to death in slow agony. Which would it be for her? Snapped neck or slow, torturous strangling?

Of course, she had not murdered anyone, nor raped the hangman's daughter like the strangling criminal. No, her crime was different. She had tried – and failed – to help a broken leg. A village draftsman had been pinned by the falling of his collapsing cart and after the rest of his team had extricated him, the men had brought him to her cabin on a stretcher with a nasty compound fracture of his upper leg. Given Gailin's reputation for having a healing touch, the townsfolk often brought her the sick to tend, but this was her first case of dealing with an otherwise healthy man. She had treated breaks before but not when the bone was completely out of position. This did not bode well for her. She probably didn't have the physical strength to even muscle the bone into place and had warned the victim's distraught wife of this possibility.

Then foolishly, she had tried to set the bone. The positioning of the break went as well as could be expected, but marrow from the bone must have gotten into his bloodstream, poisoning him. He had died in a terrible fever in Gailin's cabin two days later and when the men of the village came to collect the draftman's body, they also came to arrest her for witchcraft.

No trial for a witch, for she would put a spell on you. How else would her aging grandmother have survived so long? How else would she and those close to her have survived, without a mark, the pox that had dealt a blow to the town that winter? Gailin must be a witch and had deliberately poisoned the draftsman.

And so the next day she was to swing from the gallows like the two other criminals.

Drake could not resist a hanging, and this one boasted three ropes already set on the gallows. That his prey had come to this town and blended into the crowd was convenient, for now Drake got to enjoy the spectacle and follow his enemy into town. Perhaps the local villagers would let him dispose of the bodies...no, best not get involved. He needed to follow the Mountain Man and nothing must distract him from that pursuit. If Drake got to watch the execution so much the better. He could observe the Mountain Man easily enough from the audience and not miss a bit of the event.

The entire village must have come out for this execution. Drake watched with interest as the first criminal, hands bound behind him, was ushered up onto a stool and then had the noose placed around his neck. His crimes were read dutifully to the assembly while the criminal looked down in agony. He had been found guilty of murder, for he had beaten his wife in a drunken fit and killed her. Then, without more ceremony, the masked hangman kicked the stool out from underneath the criminal and the snap of his neck came echoing to Drake's magical ears. The sorcerer drank in the familiar wash of emotion sinking through his guts warming him through and through.

Then the hooded hangman marshaled another criminal onto the gallows. This villain showed the fear of a guilty man, Drake noted. This criminal's eyes bugged and he frantically looked over the crowd in abject hope that someone would come to his rescue. His broken nose and swollen eyes spoke volumes, for he had been beaten quite handily by someone while in custody and Drake felt each bruise as a warm spot on his own face, and licked his lips in anticipation. He watched carefully as the hangman deliberately moved the knot to the back of the criminal's neck and Drake had to stifle a chuckle. This one he could not wait to see. The crime; rape, caught in the act. Of that, Drake could care less. He wanted the stool to go skittering across the gallows. And when it did, the pleasure Drake felt almost made him melt. Each struggling gasp and kick of leg, desperate for some purchase, made the hunter feel that welcome sensation of ecstasy.

Without waiting for the rapist to actually die, the hangman went off the platform for his final victim. This one surprised even Drake, forcing him to look away from the struggling rapist. A woman? She was a delicate thing with honey gold hair and a young, innocent face, but she looked out over the crowd with steely green eyes. She was not repentant, nor afraid, but instead, resigned. Her body did not tremble, but she looked at the other two criminals, her companions in fate, with a strange fascination. Did she have the same attraction to death that Drake did? What crime could this small woman have committed to warrant such an end? Hanging a woman was so rare that Drake could not recall ever seeing it in his very long and varied experience.

The hangman retrieved his stool, had the girl step up and realized that she was simply too short even then for the noose and he had to go leave briefly to find something more to raise her up so the rope would reach. When he returned with a thick book to stand on, the girl obediently stepped up higher. The hangman pulled aside her braid so the noose would fit snuggly around her slender neck and then whispered something to her, probably apologies.

Would the height of the noose be enough to snap her neck, Drake wondered in fascination? He hoped not. He had never performed an autopsy of a woman and wanted her lovely neck to remain unbroken. Let her suffer and strangle so that he could later caress her cold neck intact and smooth as silk. Without meaning to, Drake magically shifted the knot ever so slightly to the back of her neck so no one would notice. A little sorcery went a long way to quench his pleasure and need.

The young woman's crime was read: witchcraft and Drake almost cringed. If witchcraft for failing to help an injured man was worthy of hanging, what would a full-fledged sorcerer like himself warrant? For him, they would break out a bonfire. Why hadn't they burned this girl? Not that Drake was ungrateful. A burned body of such a lovely woman would not be nearly as pleasurable to work on and he wanted to take his time with her corpse, not having to hold his breath because of the stench of burned flesh. In his native country they would have drowned her, and that would be nice if he got to her body soon enough.

Now, how was he going to get the bodies, Drake wondered greedily.

* * *

Vamilion came into the town with trepidation. Being followed by a dark sorcerer meant nothing at this point; he had been hunted for years and always found a way to escape. This, however was different. He simply had to find out what was going on here, or the niggling magical instincts that forced him from his home would drive him insane. Crossing the open land, far from the safe mountains made him restless too and while he could have traveled magically, right now he needed to be in contact with people to find the source of his instinctive itch and that meant walking instead of magically leaping. Oh, the logical part of Vamilion's brain told him he needed to keep moving to avoid a confrontation with the hunter sorcerer. He also needed to wear himself out so the magical itch would not keep him awake. So he walked three hundred miles in a week across the plain to this village on the Don River.

Walking this river for days Vamilion had passed through four towns and now found this one with every citizen out on the village green for an execution. The itch he felt only grew stronger. Restlessly he blended in with the gawkers, feeling a little sick at the spectacle they had all come to see: a hanging. However, Vamilion knew he had come to the right place. The magical itch shifted in his head, becoming almost incessant; obviously this gruesome event was what he had come to address.

Without considering it Vamilion went to the base of the gallows and ducked underneath, out of sight before reaching out with his magical instincts to find the source of this insistent pinging. He acutely felt drawn to the three criminals chained together at the steps behind where the people had gathered. The three would remain out of sight while the magistrate checked papers, advised the hangman and saw all was in order. Meanwhile Vamilion reached out to tap into the minds of each of the criminals. One, a drunk, one a rapist that almost made him want to vomit and finally, and to his surprise, Vamilion brushed his mind against that of the woman.

He lurched, and sat down with a thump in the dust under the gallows. To balance himself, he placed his hands against the ground, seeking a deep place where stone waited and felt the world settle a bit before he could concentrate again. Gailin. He had found her, despite his concerted efforts not to go Seeking her. He didn't want to find this woman. For twenty-five years he had avoided this moment, hoping it would not happen for ages more. Gailin, the woman to whom he must give the magical gift, a woman who could match his formidable talents, the woman who would be the next Wise One.

The woman who would become his wife.

Vamilion sighed with regret as his ever-present grief loomed like a mountain, crushing him. How would he explain this to Paget? If his wife who had stuck with him throughout his forays into magic could endure being supplanted, she was an angel. Could he keep this a secret from his sweet Paget? Could he keep the compulsion and attraction he would invariably experience being near Gailin from kicking in? So far, all he knew of this new lady were her feet and then that brief brush with her mind. He would not risk going any nearer, but already he felt an unmistakable urge to come investigate and rescue her. It had dragged him from hundreds of miles away, from his safe haven to come find her, with that frantic itch.

Couldn't he just let Gailin hang? Despicable as the thought might be, it would solve his problem. Eventually another Gailin would be born in another age. He would find that other one, surely. But the itch had been demanding. It was unthinkable to let any innocent die, especially since she was facing the gallows because of magic. The ethics imposed on him by his own power, the Wise One magic, would not allow it. Vamilion sighed with regret and began considering a way for him to do what he must, without putting himself in the direct face of discovery or he would find himself swinging from the gallows right beside this girl.

As the murderer was hung, Vamilion planned. The Mountain Man, Drake's prey, conjured his needs and knew exactly what to do by the time the second man had swung. Vamilion stepped out from his hiding place to stand just behind Gailin, near the back steps of the platform. Keeping his eyes closed, fearful of making eye contact with the lady, he hesitated until the hangman came down to retrieve her. Then without letting anyone actually see, he touched the hangman's arm, caught him as he fell under a sleeping spell, changed his own appearance into that of the executioner, hood and all, and shoved the sleeping man under the gallows in one swift move. Gailin did not even notice that. He then took her arm and escorted her up onto the platform.

Vamilion carefully kept his eyes on the crowd, even spying the hunter in the audience, watching for him, but he was reasonably sure his enemy was distracted by the hanging itself, so the mountain man felt he could work undetected. He gently lifted Gailin to the stool and then reached for the noose. Too short, even when she helpfully stood on tiptoe. Disconcerted by this oversight, Vamilion went back down the back of the platform and rifled through the hangman's equipment, finding nothing to help. So he conjured a book as thick as his arm and pretended to locate it in the executioner's things.

"Please step up, miss," he said solemnly. Gailin did as ordered and with seven inches shoved under her boots, Vamilion could reach up and grasp the rope. He lifted her brilliant hair to the side while trying to actually look or feel it, and placed the noose up under her chin where it almost cut into her pale skin even with the extra height. Then Vamilion secretly placed a glowing ball of Heart Stone in her hands that remained tied behind her back. He felt her turn to look at him in curiosity, but avoided her gaze and instead made sure she grasped the walnut sized orb.

"When you drop, wish for the rope to break, grab the book and then run for your life, Gailin," he whispered behind her back, as he tried not to breathe in her evocative scent of herbs.

Vamilion didn't think about what he was doing while the magistrate read off the charges of witchcraft against her. What he was about to do might even bring a worse sentence for her, but he could not shy away or the magic would prevent him from kicking the stool out from under her. Instead he faced toward the back of the gallows, looked past her up the river and wished for mountains. Then, the moment the magistrate finished, Vamilion took a deliberate step into the stool and kept walking as she fell. He hopped off the back of the platform and began running. He never heard if her feet landed and if her wishing magic would work, but now it didn't matter. He had turned her into a Wise One and his duty for now was done.

Chapter 2

Written

Gailin wished with all her might, grasping the mysterious ball the hangman had given her. Then her stomach dropped as the footstool fell away. The rope at her neck snapped above her head. Even the one around her wrists and on the two bodies of the criminals beside her severed. The wish even included the lashing that held the gallows together and it began unraveling. The platform grew unsteady as she landed on her feet, still alive. To the gasps of the crowd she slid on the teetering platform toward her fellow victims and only caught herself from being clubbed in the head by the swinging leg of a dead man by sliding all the way to the ground.

In the mayhem that ensued, she turned to see her benefactor's back as he bolted through the streets and out of town, heading north east toward the surrounding forest. She could only see his dark head and remember his words. "Run for your life, Gailin."

Run? She looked around herself at the horrified crowd and the tumbled timbers. She saw the real hangman rising out of the debris, rubbing his head and wondering what had happened to him. People in the crowd began pointing toward her and the shouts of 'witch' had only begun. If they had a slight reason for calling her a witch before she came to the gallows, then certainly this complete disaster did nothing to dispel the accusation. Her quick hands pocketed the little orb her rescuer had given her and without a second of thought she snatched up the book she had been standing on and bolted east, toward the forest after her mysterious benefactor.

* * *

For his part Drake began swearing under his breath. How had he not sensed this happening? The Mountain Man had performed more magic in the last few minutes than he had demonstrated in all the years Drake had stalked him. Now the dark sorcerer would have to run too if he were to catch his prey and what would happen then? A pitched magical battle? Drake didn't know if he could win such a contest and had survived to his ancient age by avoiding just such a situation. Instead, he used stealth and deception to work his way magically in this Land and if the Wise One was using such blatant power, something tremendous had changed. So what could Drake do instead of chasing across the countryside?

He looked to where the girl had run off and realized there lay his next move. She stood at the center of this mystery and Drake wanted to learn more of her before he did anything. So Drake approached the ruins of the gallows and found someone with whom to speak. "Excuse me, sir. What happened here?" he asked of the magistrate who was trying to examine the ropes that had unraveled. Meanwhile the rest of the men in town were gathering the wood or finding their pikes and swords to go after the girl.

"Magic, of course," the magistrate grumbled. "She put a spell on all the ropes. We were hanging her for witchcraft and this proves it. Next time we'll burn her at the stake."

"Is that wise, sir? How will you catch her?" Drake pretended innocently enough.

"She won't go far," a woman nearby commented as she was wrapping the bodies of the two criminals so the debris of the gallows could be cleared. "Her Grandmother is still alive and Gailin wouldn't leave her."

Drake stirred. He had the girl's name. If he wanted, he could call her to himself right now and put her under his spell, but that would be too obvious a magical trick and he didn't want to reveal himself quite yet, not if a bonfire were what awaited magic in this backwater village.

"Sir, where is Gailin's grandmother? I'm not from this town and she won't recognize me. If she comes back to her grandmother's home, I can send you word and you can catch her then."

"Catch her?" the magistrate scoffed. "How? We didn't know she could do this much. Usually she just heals goats and the croup. Gailin's never done something this... this... destructive."

"Except she let Kail die," the lady wrapping the bodies commented. "Now we've lost the only healer in the village."

The magistrate didn't want to hear another obvious flaw in his plan and so he pulled Drake farther away from the gallows and advised him on how to find Gailin's house, where she had been tending her grandmother until a few days before. After promising that he would inform the magistrate if Gailin returned to her home, Drake departed to find the cottage on the edge of the forest where he hoped he could lure the girl, if she did not come voluntarily. At least it had the advantage of being isolated, away from the village proper. From there he could simply call her and she would be his, heart and soul.

* * *

Jonis paced back and forth in front of the small cabin that bordered the forest edge. He couldn't stand being indoors right now, even if the house almost blended into the forest around it. Instead he appeased his guilt by keeping the door open to the late spring wind. He would hear if Gailin's grandmother stirred. It was the least he could do for the young lady he'd fallen in love with.

Grieving silently, Jonis trod back and forth from the kitchen garden on the southern side to the well-worn path weaving into the thinning forest. He had heard about the hanging and knew exactly what

14

Gailin would have asked of him if he had been there when she was arrested: please watch over Grandmother and don't come to see the hanging. He had known Gailin all his life and while he could never actually say the words aloud, he loved her. Now his love was too late.

Grandmother, the only family Gailin ever had, rarely woke and Jonis had avoided answering the old woman's quavering questions whenever she did wake by feeding her the broth that the girl had left in the pot, but he could not bear speaking the words of truth to the grandmother. Gailin's hanging would kill Grandmother and Jonis couldn't face more death at this point. Nothing was going to be the same with Gailin gone.

Jonis looked up into the sky, glaring at the high noon sun. It would be done by now. Hung for helping. He could not believe the village would do such a thing. Primitive as they were how could anyone say an evil bone existed in Gailin's makeup? Miserably Jonis finally got together the nerve to go back into the hut, out from under the betraying noon sun to wait for Grandmother to waken and to share with her finally, the fate of her granddaughter.

* * *

Drake approached the rustic cabin cautiously. He didn't want to frighten the girl if she had already come back home. He pushed his magical awareness ahead of him and sensed two people in the cabin, one in bed, one upright but he could not guess at more.

Therefore he would come as an expected visitor and walked up to the door to knock. People in this land were suspicious of many things but manners went a long way to reassuring them.

"Hello? Is anyone home?" he called and then stuck his head inside.

Only a small fire on the hearth lit the low, single room cottage and beyond the table Drake saw a young man who paced back and forth. From his distracted look he probably was a farmer in the local area, neglecting his fields at planting season out of devotion to his sweetheart by watching over her grandmother. The dirt and sweat on his clothes made it seem like he had come directly from the fields and his distress etched itself on his face. But as Drake walked in, it seemed the young man might crumble.

"Did they… did they…?" the young man began, his voice cracking.

Drake came into the hut and held out a hand. "Relax, young man. Gailin escaped. She sent me here to tell you, for she will not be able to come back. She wanted me to check on her grandmother. Now, what's your name, boy?"

"J…Jonis."

"Well Jonis, I'm here to help. Has Gailin returned yet?"

Jonis gave him one confused look and Drake easily read in his simple mind; Gailin didn't even know how her beau had gallantly come to defend her home, anything to soften the blow for her.

16

And Gailin would never know, even now. Drake would not leave Jonis to interfere with what he now planned. The magician's green, careful eyes flicked a look at the old woman asleep in the bed beyond and then took a step toward the young farmer.

"Well, if she hasn't returned, then it's not too late." Drake felt his mouth move into a false smile. His clever eyes caught the simple dirt brown stare of the confused peasant and reached out his hand toward him to say, without a bit of inflection, "Jonis, die."

The farmer's head rolled back faster than his eyes, his knees buckling and he went down, obedient to the sorcerer's order. A sack of his own grain held more life than the bag of burly bones the young man represented while Drake soaked in yet another life force, strong and vibrant. The sorcerer trembled with pleasure and luxuriated in the warmth it brought to his gut. Then, without any ceremony, he made the earthen floor of the cabin swallow the farmer whole. Let him fertilize here rather than out in his fields somewhere.

Drake then turned to the old woman who slept on in oblivion. Taking her life, flickering and fading, would benefit nothing and might make Gailin suspicious. While he had every intention of using the girl, he wanted her willingly, not frightened or coerced magically. Wouldn't that be a feat: to command a magician without force?

So Drake would wait just as Jonis had, for Gailin to come home. The wizard might even walk the same path back and forth, pressing the disturbed earthen floor, just in case it appeared like someone was buried there. Drake could wait patiently.

* * *

At dusk Vamilion stopped his stealthy path through the forest, pausing at a creek that ran through the trees to rest and take his bearings. He needed to listen to the magic that moved around him. He could sense the dark sorcerer had given up the search for him, having remained behind in the village. The girl, the new Wise One, she had survived her hanging and Vamilion's awkward attempt to rescue her. Vamilion magically sensed how she had followed him into the forest, though she had fallen several miles behind, and had also stopped for the evening. He could practically taste her fear and confusion. Well, that meant he could continue to help her after a fashion. He only hoped this worked.

Vamilion drew on the magic he possessed to conjure a fire, a bucket in which to put water and a quick meal all while he found a mossy stone under the trees to serve as a seat. Then with a bit more concentration he conjured a tablet with a blackwood stylus to match it. He had never actually done this, but until he trained Gailin, hopefully from a distance, he had a responsibility to help her. He would not leave her in this new magical world to stumble into her powers as his mentor had done to him.

Tapping into his imagination, Vamilion crafted a link between the tablet he held and the book that Gailin hopefully still carried with her. Creating that link after the fact was difficult magic. Could the girl even read? That wasn't a guarantee in this newly colonized land, full of pioneers and little opportunity to study a more civilized art like reading. If she couldn't read or write, this effort to teach from a distance just got more difficult. Slowly, with the flickering firelight as his guide, Vamilion began writing on his tablet with the stylus and imagined the book in the girl's possession reflected his message. He then sculpted a yearning for her to look into the book and discover its secrets.

Hopefully her curiosity would guide her. Gailin had stopped in the forest and found a place to rest, curling up around her pit of fear, though she would never be able to sleep after the scare she had experienced. Vamilion imagined her staring wide-eyed up through the branches of the forest at the full moon overhead and would feel the tickling desire to explore the prize she had taken with her. She would sit up in the twilight and open the book, brushing her hands across the blank pages and then see how his words seeped onto the first page, line by careful line. She would want to know about the magic that had rescued, and then abruptly abandoned her. It would be in her nature as a Wise One to want to know more.

That same curiosity ran through his own veins and had driven Vamilion to come to this newly opened land twenty-five years before. And that curiosity had brought Owailion to him and made him a magician before he even knew what that meant. The first Wise One, Owailion, had given him no choice but to touch the Heart Stone, no more than Vamilion had just given to Gailin in her turn. It was cruel to have no choice, but this new nation, the Land and its unbridled magic demanded it. Where there flowed power, there must be some way to harness it or the wild magic would escape and forever scar the Land.

Vamilion wrote carefully, "If you can read this, please write back to me."

Then he waited, not daring to tap into Gailin's thoughts, to see if she had given in to the prompting and opened the book or even noticed his message. She had camped only a few miles away, well within his ability to hear her mind, but that did not tempt him. He would not do that if he could help it. Listening to her thoughts would only bring the compulsion to love her all the stronger. He must avoid that urge with all his might. He wanted to be faithful to Paget, no matter what magic might demand of him. Vamilion would fight to remain Paget's husband.

He waited, imagining the girl finding a burnt stick or a rock in the ground that she could gouge out a corresponding message back to him. It might take half the evening, but he could be patient. But what if she couldn't read? Could he teach her from afar? Probably not, but he could hope before he considered what he would do if she lacked that skill. Patience was another talent a Wise One must command and Vamilion possessed more than even he knew. He could wait for the foundations of stone to erode away if need be and not stir if magic demanded the patience of a mountain.

Gailin couldn't run anymore and her fear and confusion only added to the exhaustion. The dark of the forest, even though the sun had not yet set, contributed as well. Hunger and chill also made their demands known and she had to sit. Without meaning to, she slumped down against a tree trunk and finally stopped her escape. Had she been obedient enough to the order to run for her life? She would lose her life if she continued much farther.

Without the frantic roar of her heart and her own breathing in her ears, she could hear water nearby and turned an ear toward the sound. She crawled the few feet to the brook and drank her fill, heedless of the impurities she knew lurked there. When she finally had the energy to move again, though her arms trembled at the effort to leverage herself away from the water, she looked around and began to assess her situation.

Frankly, her world was gone. She dare not return to her home; the villagers would stake that out immediately, knowing she would worry about her grandmother. Would Jonis come watch over her grandmother? He would have done that last service for her, even if she had spurned his advances. She couldn't remember seeing his kind face in the crowd at the hanging and she doubted he would have the stomach for such a horrible spectacle. Now, looking back with regret, she knew it had been wise to cut his love out of her life. Being a farmer's wife had never figured into her future and she had known it even before the boy had come to her cabin with a bouquet of wildflowers and all the sweet words he could mumble.

But Gailin would not survive long in the woods alone and without a single tool to her name. She looked around herself and noticed the frayed end of the noose still around her neck. Almost frantically she clawed off the obscene necklace and then examined the break in the rope with a clinical eye. Every strand had burst on its own, not in a clean cut but in a tremendous, raggedy rip. What force had done this? Well, she couldn't answer that so she began dismantling the rope, strand for strand as she considered possibilities.

Magic, of course had been behind her miraculous escape, but what kind of magic? Her grandmother had told her of the magic in Malornia where she had come from originally and how dragons and demons lurked throughout that country, making the wilds dangerous beyond belief. The non-magical humans there needed to congregate in great cities to avoid destruction. The magical people had protected them, but had also ruled with an iron fist, controlling those without the gifts, almost like slaves. No one dared venture far from the walled cities and so starvation and disease often stalked the crowded streets.

That was why Grandma had immigrated to this country. The Land had been sealed for time in memorial and no humans had settled until the time of the Breaking, when suddenly, for no known reason, the Land had opened. People like Gailin's grandparents had come to settle in this newly opened but utterly wild territory. They might not have the protection of walls and magic, but at least they were free to make their own way. Unfortunately, the diseases of the old lands had followed the immigrants, and taken Gailin's parents before she ever knew them. Raised by her grandmother on the tales from the old lands, the golden-headed girl had sworn to learn how to battle disease without magic. That was why they had settled here, near a river, along a forest with the prairie on the edge and the mountains only a few days walk away. She gathered all the herbs and mushrooms needed to cure the worst diseases. She also grew the rich garden that provided all the nutrients to remain healthy that could be found here.

That the villagers distrusted her healthy ways could not be helped. The settlers had brought with them the suspicions from their old lands too. While no one here seemed born with magic, the stories and fears of such power existed and poisoned many who came. If Gailin and her grandmother so much as weathered the yearly flu without misery, the cry of magic went through the village. So now Gailin sat in the dark dismantling the rope that evidenced that distrust. She looked down at the strands of hemp now filling her filthy apron and considered them bitterly. Could she weave this mess into a more serviceable rope? She needed something with which to catch food and it might prove to be a decent snare at least.

She had only begun to weave her snare when the compulsion to look at the book struck like a spear.

She couldn't see the tome clearly in the dark, but her need to open the thick cover drove her to it. Her grandmother had taught her the value of books and had laboriously taught her the letters, but the only book she had ever seen was her grandmother's herb and plant book. She had marveled at the delicately drawn and colored pictures, paying little attention to the words written carefully below each image. Now she eagerly lifted the hefty new book and then looked around the trees for her best light. She ended up sitting under a dead tree that boasted no leaves and so allowed the light of the full moon to filter down. Then she lifted the cover.

The creamy pages glowed brilliantly under the moonlight, without a mark on them. No pictures or words marred their surface. She was about to turn to the next empty page when, much to her surprise, a firmly written word began to appear. One simple sentence emerged across the first page, as if her perusal had instigated the magic to make it appear. It emerged slowly, in strong, simple enough script for her to work out the words in her rudimentary skill.

"If you can read this, write back to me."

If I can read this? How could she hope to write back? Who was doing this? The hangman who had rescued her, surely? Magic again threw its weight back at her, tossing her into that world and she couldn't find her bearings. This magic, so unlike the tales of blasts and bloodletting, explosions and evil her grandmother had told her, haunted Gailin now. Dare she answer back? She knew deep down that this magic demanded she answer it but she had nothing with which to reply. She looked around at the forest floor and wondered. The dead tree against which she rested might have bark that rotted and would leave a mark on the white page. With her fingers she gouged a longish strip out of the softened bark and experimentally drew it along her palm. The material crumbled into a thick bumbling mark, but if she sharpened it a bit against the ground, working off the weaker bits, it might make a readable letter.

"I can read a little. Who are you?" she wrote carefully, filling the opposite page with her thick, choppy bark scratches.

Her mystery correspondent replied back almost immediately, but elected to move his much thinner, finely written words to the next page so as to not interfere with her childish script. "I'm the one who told you to wish the rope to break. You may call me Vamilion. It's not my real name, but it is not safe to use names. I know yours so do not write it here. In fact, do not use your name again. It will never be safe for you to use your name."

Gailin scrawled the obvious, "Why?"

"You will have many questions," he wrote below her crumbling script. "First, let's get you a better writing stick. Much like you wished the rope to break, you can wish for a stylus. Think about the ground beneath you. Imagine there is a writing stick in your hand and concentrate. Then wish the matter of the earth would turn into that writing device and put it in your hand."

Gailin wasn't at all satisfied with this surreal message, but she also felt the lure of a challenge. Was she becoming a magician, or was this mystery man doing the magic and all she was doing was the wishing? She felt willing to experiment at least. She held out her hand above the book and closed her eyes, concentrating on the humus on the forest floor. Some bit of it would gather into graphite and charcoal, coalescing into a stick easily sharpened to a fine tip. It took her a moment to focus on this wish and then she felt the shaft appear in her hand and her eyes flashed open with amazement.

Breathlessly she wrote, demonstrating her success with her much improved handwriting. "Can this wishing provide me with a supper? I've not eaten in over a day."

"Yes," Vamilion wrote back. "Very good. A stylus is easy, but conjuring anything you need is relatively simple magic. Be careful though. You might attract attention if you conjure too many grand things that aren't strictly necessary. Usually you make do with what everyone else around you must use."

"Supper?" Gailin wrote back and then set the stylus in between the pages and practiced this new skill by bringing into being a plate of vegetables steamed and a bit of rabbit already cooked in the herbs she knew tasted best. She had to concentrate more, for her hands trembled in her nervous realization that this man had turned her into a magician.

"Are you doing this, or am I?" she asked awkwardly with one hand shoveling food into her mouth and the other trying to write. She had to turn the page to read his reply, but he finally began to explain, having realized that she would pepper him with questions for the remainder of the night if he didn't explain quickly.

"You are now a magician. That globe I gave you on the gallows is called a Heart Stone. It is the key to magic in this Land. You are a Wise One, a magician of the Land. There are relatively few people here who can tap into magic here. In fact, you are the third of sixteen who will eventually protect the Land and seal it from outside magic and invasion. As such, you are now going to live forever, but you will have to sacrifice your will to the good of the people. Unlike in other kingdoms, magic here will only flow to those who are naturally gifted for it and who hold to the magic-directed values that only God will allow. That is what the Heart Stone will demand of you. You will find it impossible to even lie or do other evil now. But because of those restrictions, you will be a more powerful magician than in other lands like Marewn, Demion or Malornia. There the magic is widespread but it does not flow freely and one must use spells, demons and blood sacrifice to invoke it. And the magicians there naturally lust for more and more power. It will eventually corrupt them."

Gailin watched the gentle etching of lead spreading across the page and wondered at this turn in her life. One day she was going to be hung for magic that wasn't real and the next she found herself with more magical power than she could even comprehend. She set the plate aside and picked up the stylus before Vamilion could continue.

"Why me?"

Vamilion must have been hesitating on his side of the correspondence, for his reply did not emerge until after she had finally finished her meal and picked up the stylus again, wondering if he had fallen asleep on the other end.

"God gave me your name," Vamilion wrote frankly. "He selected you and I found you. It is how the next Wise One is chosen."

That reply left more questions than it answered, but she managed to pare it down to just one at a time. "And why are we writing in this book instead of you telling me this in person? You ran from me."

Again Vamilion's reply waited a painfully long time and Gailin feared she would fall asleep before he replied. Finally she almost wanted to turn the book into a pillow, for she could hardly keep her eyes open to read. The moon had set and she had no light or guidance to consider making a lantern. But eventually he replied. "It is best this way. You are tired. We will write again in the morning."

Chapter 3

Compulsion

How she managed to sleep well into the morning, she never knew, but Gailin woke with the sun bright in her eyes and her muscles sore beyond anything she could remember. She must have run hours yesterday and after the terror of almost being hung and then finding magic was real in her life; well, she could understand if her body forced her to suffer. She must have conjured a blanket for herself, for she brushed off a covering she didn't really remember creating and wondered if it was all a dream. Well, one way to find out.

She looked at her 'camp' that consisted of the blanket at the base of a dead tree and a book for a pillow. Could she prove that Vamilion and his wondrous promise of magic were real? Could she make herself breakfast without his instruction? Warily, fearing it would not work, she reached out toward the ground and wished a fire into being. Kindling obediently popped out of the ground like dandelions and then collapsed under the weight of heavier wood and then the pile burst into flames. Her smile appeared just as magically.

The fire was only for comfort. She conjured an already cooked plate of eggs and toast, sat down at her fire to eat it and then considered what she had learned. In a way she knew so little, she felt like she was trying to diagnose someone whose only symptom was a headache. It could be as simple as stress or as deadly as a tumor. She needed to know more to dispel her fear. All the implied power but none of the direction had been forthcoming. Could she really live forever? Was there a consequence to tapping into all this wishing? Why must she not use her name? Why was Vamilion running away from her and yet trying to teach her using the book as a go between? And what were they both fleeing? He had told her to run for her life. Why was that?

With a full stomach and no direction, Gailin picked up the book, expecting to review the previous night's dialog, but to her surprise, the pages were as white and clear as new-fallen snow once again. One would think her entire encounter with Vamilion was a dream, but for her obvious skill in conjuring. Gailin snatched up her stylus that had not disappeared and began with that question. "Where is everything we wrote last night?" and then launched into a dozen more questions she wanted answered. If Vamilion wasn't going to come and teach her, she would at

least act the dutiful student and find answers somehow.

Suddenly she felt her hand freeze midway through
the word she wrote. "Gailin, stop writing," she heard
in her head. Alarmed, she looked up and then saw
new words appear below hers.

"I can't reply while you're writing," Vamilion
wrote. "You have to give me a chance to answer."

She had not considered that, and wrote a brief
apology and then added "How did you stop me?"

"That is one of the most dangerous forms of magic.
Its name magic. If a magician – any magician- knows
your name he can command you to do anything, like
forcing you to stop writing. That's why I told you
to never use your name again. There are evil magicians we call sorcerers, stalking me…probably you
now too, who have enough power to command you
to do anything. It's how the Queen of Rivers died."

Gailin didn't write anything in reply for she recognized the pause might be that Vamilion was upset with that statement. When he continued, his
hand looked a little unsteady and his handwriting
grew smaller, tighter. "She was the second Wise One.
Owailion, the first Wise One did not know about
name magic and so didn't warn her to protect her
name. The sorcerers on the other side of the Seal
heard her name and used it to manipulate her. Eventually she used name magic on herself and commanded herself to die rather than harm the Land
and the people she loved. It was some of her final magic
that broke the Seal in the first place. Either that or

31

the last command she obeyed was to break the Seal which opened the Land to immigration...and invasion by foreign magic."

A sense of panic began to sink down Gailin's spine. "Can you help me avoid that? Everyone in the village knows my name. My grandmother, she's not well and she's probably alone. I must go to help her."

"No, you cannot go back." Vamilion must have felt her panic and pain, for he continued almost immediately. "But yes, I can help you. I can help you build your mind into a fortress. After the skill of conjuring, shielding out minds while reading others, it's our most fundamental magical skill. It's vital to protect your thoughts from manipulation by this evil. There was one of those sorcerers at the hanging yesterday. I'm afraid that's why I ran. I had hoped that he would follow me and not even realize that you were also a Wise One at that point. It failed, but it was worth a try."

"So why are you still running? Can you go and help my grandmother, if I cannot?" Gailin wrote frantically.

She waited for Vamilion's reply but the white page remained blank and she grew impatient. "You know I will just go myself. One or the other of us must go see to my grandmother and she knows me."

"Don't manipulate me, woman."

The words practically growled at her from the page and she suspected he was speaking in her head again, for she felt his frustration with this dilemma. Reluctantly she waited for him to think about what she had said. Of course someone needed to go tend to her grandmother. If there was a sorcerer out there seeking for the both of them and Gailin's name was free out in the wind, something must be done. She had no idea how magic might help her grandmother but she suspected Vamilion did. She wanted to know what he was thinking. Could she listen in on his thoughts too?

Feeling her way through the book, Gailin let her mind wander, imagining Vamilion as a stranger; dark haired and mysterious, huddled under a tree in the deepest depth of the forest with a book in his lap but his mind far away as he considered the possibilities. She felt drawn to him and wondered if her imagination had tapped into the truth of him. She daydreamed his real voice would be the same as his mental one; gravely and comfortable with the pain behind the words. It wasn't a soothing thought. Little knowing what she was doing, she crafted this new magical link, reaching out, hoping she would at least hear something.

"If I go," Vamilion thought, "I will have to battle him and there will be time in a fight. It will only take a just a snap of thought to kill her. But if I let her go to tend her grandmother, the sorcerer might sense the magic on her. Can I teach her to protect herself enough to not seem magical and maybe he won't suspect what she really is? He won't even think to manipulate her. Can she learn that much magic without more intense training? She'll need to learn it eventually, but then I'll have to get close. I cannot avoid

33

the compulsion if I get close enough to teach her. How many years can she endure without training? Could I get Owailion to train her instead? And that still leaves her grandmother."

Gailin couldn't resist adding her own thought. "If I didn't use magic, just went home like nothing happened, would any sorcerer even know who I was?"

"!"

Something hard and blank slammed up in front of Gailin's startled imagination. All she could sense out in the forest was a wall, high and forbidding. Unfazed, she picked up the stylus and wrote in terse words back. "What was that?"

She had to wait for the slow, tedious words to arrive on the page, but at least he was willing to reply. "That was what I intended to teach you next; me blocking you out. You must not listen into my mind and I won't listen into yours unless you allow me access. It's dangerous ....and rude."

She sighed before she replied. "I can understand that it is rude, and I'm sorry. But why would listening to your thoughts be dangerous as well?"

This answer took more time than she expected. They were allies weren't they?

"Yes, we are more than allies, but..." he wrote, and she realized he had listened into her mental comments again. "But it will become a compulsion."

And again there came the pause, as if he had to consider his words with such care that he almost did not dare trust the book with them. Eventually he wrote and she wished suddenly that she could read

34

his body language and hear his actual words to judge why this came so painfully.

"The compulsion is magical. You will be drawn to love me and I will have no choice but to love you as well. It is natural in Wise One magic, but it is also wrong that you will not have the freedom to choose for yourself. If we don't formally meet, my hope is that the compulsion will not be as strong, or as immediate and we can resist it."

"That's another reason I ran," he continued. "I fled you, and I'm sorry. Gailin, you deserve to have the freedom to pick your life, as far as the magic will allow. I was given no choice about becoming a magician and neither were you really. If I had the chance to stop that hanging and discuss what would happen to your life before I gave you the Heart Stone, turning you into a magician, you might have chosen a normal life instead. I couldn't give you that choice. So now I will fight for whatever other choices are left: your loves, for example. The compulsion to help people, the drive to go Seeking your gifts, that cannot be stopped now. Even the inspired ideas on how to handle difficult situations come from magic. We are called Wise Ones because of these compulsions, but at least in your loves, you should still have some choice."

Gailin had no words for that reply. Vamilion sounded so unhappy with the all that power. Why would it be such a miserable life, helping people and wandering magically through the wonders of the Land? What adventures must he have enjoyed?

He could live forever and could have anything he wanted.

"Except Paget," he wrote.

Again he had listened to her thoughts rather than the words she had not written as she considered his dilemma.

"Paget?"

"She is my wife. She came with me to the Land, along with our two children. When Owailion met us at the Breaking of the Seal he didn't explain any of this to me. He didn't have any time as we were under attack. I took the Heart Stone thinking it would help us, but instead it is tearing us apart. Paget is essentially old enough to be my mother now and continues to age while I stay the way I was that day over thirty years ago. Paget ages, gets sick and even bored despite all I can give her because I have to hide her away lest the sorcerers and demons I deal with harm her. She also knows about the compulsion that will draw me to another magician and she knows that someday I would meet someone else...meet you and would be drawn and..."

Gailin waited for the words to continue, but they didn't and she felt her own way through what he was trying not to say. "And you want to remain faithful to her?"

She could almost hear his sigh of regret. "Yes, fidelity is part of the make-up of all Wise Ones. We are essentially good people, not tempted or corrupted by the power we are given. That is why it is so rare a gift. However, it brings with it pain. Paget knows this and while she trusts me, my children have grown and left us, bitter at the awkward thought that I am younger than they are. They realize I have no way to stop her dying eventually. Paget has made hints that I should leave her and go Seek as the compulsion demands. Sometimes I give in. For example, I couldn't resist the itch to come and find you before you were hung, but I will still go back to her and watch over her as she slowly ages and dies in my arms."

For the longest time Gailin could think of nothing to reply and didn't dare reach her mind out in case he had let down the wall he had created around his thoughts and she would hear the pain there. So she had discovered that although the magic seemed ultimately powerful, drawbacks abounded. She could not imagine what he was feeling, but she sensed that she would be weeping for him if she knew him just a little bit better. She would want to comfort him and....and was that the compulsion of which he spoke? If so, she swallowed a shiver of fear. She hadn't officially set eyes on the man and already she wanted to comfort him and somehow ease his burden. What a powerful spell. What would it be like when they finally met formally? Or was this desire to help just a general thing, meant for all the people she encountered now? In any case she must break the spell and encourage her mentor to teach her more.

Carefully she scratched out a few more words. "It's probably good for me to learn how to block thoughts, isn't it?"

It took him a bit before he had gathered himself to reply. "Yes, that's for the best. Normally we would do this with me trying to get past your barrier but I don't think that's wise right at this point. So let's try with you getting past my shields and you'll learn from that how to craft shields for yourself."

They spent the remainder of the morning working from that distance on shielding the mind from magical invasion. Gailin learned how to protect herself behind a wall that didn't seem magical, but might have been purely instinct and how to project her voice into the mind of others. This second skill, while valuable, would not be safe if she intended to go back to her house. What if she found a sorcerer there waiting for her? She had to appear, at least on the surface, as only somewhat gifted, like the minor sorcerers in Marewn or the untrained, apprentice magicians in Demonia who had not yet bonded with demons that would enhance their gift.

"You will encounter many different levels of magic, from many sources. It is better to know about them and be able to observe their motives, weaknesses and strengths without being judged for yourself as a magician. A good solid shield will protect you without seeming overtly magical. In fact some non-magical people have shielded thoughts. It will be naturally what anyone who wants to protect their name would use. Watch them and then let the Wise One instincts guide your decisions," Vamilion assured her.

"Well, right now my instincts are telling me to go home. Is that right, or is this the compulsion speaking?" she wrote back.

"There are different types of compulsion too. As a Wise One the good instincts, to help and be of service, are clean and while you might not know their cause, you will not feel duress if you fight them. It's almost like hunger. You want to do something about it but you can wait and resist if you are willing to ignore the itch. On the other hand, a magically demanding compulsion, like your name being invoked feels...like...I don't know, now that I think about it. How did you feel when I told you to run for your life?"

"Like I couldn't resist, that I had no choice in the matter. I couldn't stop unless I died."

"Exactly," Vamilion replied. "If you have no choice, it is magically driven and not your Wise One instincts. No other magic in this world will give you a choice, but the compulsion of the Wise Ones..."

"Even the one that will draw us toward each other?" she asked carefully.

"Yes, that too can be resisted. Owailion still feels his compulsion toward his wife, the Queen of Rivers I told you about, but he is resisting it. He would just as easily do what she did; speak his true name, if he knows it, and command himself to die. But he resists. It makes him irritable and not very friendly, but he resists."

"What other compulsions have you experienced," she asked, eagerly, hoping for something that wasn't so grim.

"Well, I've already told you of the drive to help others. Then there is the compulsion to go Seeking. There are Talismans of our power that have been hidden throughout the Land. We alone can find and use them. I have a rock pick and a sword that were hidden, waiting for me in the mountains. They have magical gifts as well as their strength that I have used to help settle the Land and drive off evil magic. Also, my yearnings are for the mountains and stone; that also might be considered a compulsion. We call it an affinity. The earth speaks to me and I am drawn to its power. I feel its pain when it quakes and I go and comfort the mountains. And so I am called the King of Mountains."

"Like the lady that died was Queen of Rivers?"

"Exactly. And before you ask, you let your wall down again and I know what you're going to write. No, I don't know where your gifts reside. That is another thing you are Seeking."

"What else?" she asked, realizing that she might need an eternal life to accomplish all that this Seeking demanded of her. Or to get used to keeping her wall of shields up even in her sleep.

"You will also look for a pendant that opens the door to a palace somewhere in the Land. It will be yours and befits the title of Queen, though the idea of ruling is completely wrong. We are not rulers. We are masters of the magic of some aspect of nature or magic itself. Rivers and Mountains, while they have hidden power, they don't need to be ruled per se," he replied.

"What is Owailion the King of?"

"He is probably best considered the King of Creation. He doesn't have any true focus unless it is crafting things. His Seeking tasks involved building those palaces for the rest of us, creating and then hiding the Talismans the rest of us must find."

"So he makes the compulsions then?"

"No, he is manipulated by them just as we are. In fact without a way to be with his wife, he really is a slave in that sense. He cannot escape it though he would probably want to. He won't be released from that compulsion until the earth ends or perhaps when all the Wise Ones have become Seated."

"Seated? You mean, when we have found our palaces and Talismans and everything?"

"Yes, the Land will, according to legend, be sealed again and we will have peace from all outside magic."

Gailin was about to ask if the compulsions would end, when she suddenly felt a tug at her heart and gasped. She had only written two words when she realized that she *had* to go see her grandmother and dropped the stylus to do just that. She had to go. Some small part of her brain realized that she was being forced, that this was exactly what they had feared. Could she manage to tell Vamilion? Her mind shrieked, even as she made the incredible effort to pick up the stylus and book before she began walk-

41

ing with deliberate steps back the way she had come the day before.

"He's calling me!" she cried out, using the newly minted skills they'd been practicing all afternoon.

For one paralyzing second she heard and felt nothing from Vamilion.

"Can you take the book with you?" she heard in her mind and sighed with relief. Vamilion wouldn't abandon her in this, now that their worst scenario had just occurred.

"Yes, but I cannot look at it. I'm walking west, not even following the river. Please help me." As she said this Gailin didn't realize she could weep in her thoughts but she could feel the tears burning at the back of her eyes. No one should be forced, especially by an evil power, just because her name was known. What awaited her?

"Relax, Gailin, and think." Vamilion's mind voice rumbled through her, buffing away the jagged edges of her panic. "Now, you know this area. How long, walking at the pace you're at, will it take to reach your home?"

Vamilion had not used name magic to calm her, but nonetheless she did begin to relax a bit as ordered. She walked with the setting sun in her eyes and considered his question. "Probably three hours. It's going to get dark soon and I won't be able to see well in this forest. Will I be able to stop to rest or sleep?"

"I don't know, but I will follow with you. I'm behind you now, and trying to catch up. Let's use this time to plan, shall we. I think this can work for us.

We know he has your name but he hasn't killed you. That's a good thing. That probably means he doesn't know you're a Wise One… at least I don't think he does. He suspects you're magic, but he wouldn't have dared this bold of a move if he knew or even guessed that you are as powerful as me. That's not his style. This hunter/sorcerer watches, waits, assesses and perhaps reports back to someone Outland. Give him as little magic to see as you can. Let him believe that you are not the one who broke your bonds, that it was me. But remember, you cannot lie to him."

"Cannot lie…How?" Her own mental voice sounded again on the verge of panic. "If I won't be able to use magic or lie to him, how can I protect myself or my grandmother if he only has to tell me to die? He will know the minute I don't have anything to say and…"

"Gailin, breathe. It's going to take your most careful thought. He doesn't know you and you don't know him. He will probably not let you see his magic either. He's subtle. He'll be all helpful and probably kinder at first than you would suspect. He won't want to frighten you. In his mind you're a little rabbit coming into his snare and he doesn't want to startle you. He will want you alive, trapped and perhaps frightened, but he won't hurt you. He must not know that you are actually a powerful bear he has captured. I will remain outside his sensing range, helping you as I can. When you know how to get past his shields or maybe even his true name, then we can strike. Now let's practice things you can say without lying.

How will you explain a blank book that you write in?"

It took only a moment to realize she had a ready answer. "A friend gave it to me. I will use it to record my findings in the forest; herbs and such. I always wanted to draw the plants I have gathered and experiment with them as medicines or supplements to flavor foods."

"Perfect. See, you are already receiving the inspiration that comes with being a Wise One. Now, how will that help you?"

"I'll be able to keep the book with me and it won't look strange if I write in a blank book or look back on previous pages. Can you write to me so he cannot see?"

"If he is there when you read it, no. He will sense it as magic coming near him, not just yours... just like he will be able to sense my thoughts toward you unless I shield them terribly close, but if I write at odd times and then allow what I write to disappear after you've read them it will still look like a blank book. I can give you a compulsion to read them, but anything else will be obvious. Now, I've been thinking about how this can work to our advantage. If he's a sorcerer, and he knows that you are magical as well, maybe you can get him to teach you what I don't dare. Challenge him to a dual of the minds, once he admits that he has magic. He will teach you to shield as well as attack. The skill is the same, no matter that he's evil."

"Is that safe? What if he breaks into my mind? Won't he...he...see you there?" she asked.

"You haven't seen me at all, remember. He'll be looking for me and all he'll see is what you have seen; me running away. He won't think to look in the book, which I am now filling with a few drawings and commentary on plants, like you suggested. Feel free to add more, but be aware, mine aren't coming from any true plant knowledge."

Gailin felt herself smile at Vamilion's frank admission. She didn't think she would be able to smile, not while her legs moved her inexorably toward certain danger and possible death. The sun had set and she found herself stumbling and reaching out to steady herself against tree trunks but she held fast to the book as if her life depended on it. Perhaps it did.

"Now, there are a few more things I have not been able to tell you that might come up. Whatever you do, you must not make him any promises or oaths. Use words like 'alright' rather than 'yes', or nod rather than admit to anything," Vamilion instructed. In the back of his mind she could hear his running pace as he trotted to catch up with her, running at an oblique angle so he would not get too close but would arrive at his closest approach before she reached her home.

"Why must I not make any promises or oaths?" she asked, wishing she could stop and rest for a bit.

"He will know that you are a Wise One if you do. When we make a solemn oath or vow...it changes us. Someday you'll see. We appear as the King or Queen we are, fit to live in one of those grand palaces and this change in appearance will be instant. He'll know and you'll be discovered. I would show you, but I don't think that's wise. Other compulsions would kick in if I tried, and we don't need that as a complication. Just trust me that you cannot promise him anything."

"I trust you, Vamilion," she whispered aloud even as she sent him the message mentally as well. And she did, though she had little reason to believe anything she had experienced recently. Indeed the whole last three days seemed surreal. She would wake up in her bed, with her grandmother in the other bed, her chores waiting for her in the spring garden and all would be well: no angry villagers calling her a witch, no hangman's noose around her neck, no sorcerers casting spells on her, no… She looked down at the book clutched in her arms. No Vamilion or his magic? He was too real, too concrete to be a dream. She knew he was real even if she had not seen his face.

"Another thing," he interrupted her thoughts that for once she had carefully kept behind her shield. "We need to make the Heart Stone disappear. He might not know what it does but you won't be able to explain it and it's obviously magical."

"If I dropped it here in the forest, could you find it again?" she asked, but wondered if she could even summon the will to reach into her pocket and fetch out the marble he had given her on the gallows.

"No… well, yes I could find it but you separating from it would not be wise. The Heart Stone must remain with you. It is where the magic flows and it acts as a judge. If he ordered you to do something evil with your magic, it should prevent you, even above the name magic. And it can act as a guide just like the book. If I left you a message in the Heart Stone, he wouldn't even know. All you need to do is touch it. Can you make it invisible?"

"I can try," she replied warily. Here she was, stumbling around in the dark, tripping over tree roots, clutching a book and trying to fish her Heart Stone out of her pocket without dropping either of her precious possessions. It took her supreme concentration. She found the orb in her pocket and drew it out, wondering if her wish could make it disappear. She held it out, grateful for its soft glow, almost enough to light her way, but she was about to make it fade. She set her wish on it and watched the light blink out and the dark descend again, though she felt it still in her palm. With regret she dropped it back into her pocket.

"It's done," she called to Vamilion. "Can you sense it with me?"

"No, but that's a good thing. Only you know where it is. Now, can you tell how near you are to your house? I don't dare come much closer."

"How do I do that? I don't think I can do magic with all this stomping through the trees and…" Gailin could sense her panic inhibiting even her mind link to Vamilion, somewhere just north of her.

Vamilion's deep voice calmed her, made her compartmentalize her fear into a separate portion of her brain and she could hear him give her precise instructions. "Reach out your mind, like when you were trying to reach for me. Instead, reach toward your grandmother. You know her and can sense if she's there. Can you judge the distance?

It would have been easier if she could stop walking and close her eyes to concentrate on this little act of magic. She wouldn't have been able to recognize anything here in the dark, off her familiar paths even if she was already in her garden, but doing so with magic meant little to her now. She did indeed close her eyes, holding one hand out in front of her so that she wouldn't run into a tree as she threw her mind forward, stretching and flowing like fresh water across the terrain. As if she could see it, she felt a gentle push. Her mind and hand were the same. She could feel the texture of wood, the flicker of a fire set to trim the night's chill and wondered at the scent of a stew somewhere near…too near.

"It's very close," she gasped and drew her impressions back into her mind. "I'll be there in moments. Are you too near?"

Vamilion's reply gave her a different kind of comfort. "Don't fret about me. Can you tell how many people are there? Your grandmother? You need the experience of hearing some other mind than mine. Be careful to not touch the sorcerer's mind."

Obediently Gailin moved her thoughts to the north east corner of the cabin where her grandmother's bed could be nearest the fire. She wove through the thick wood logs of the wall and found the dim, hazy thoughts of her ancient grandmother, dreaming of the warm hearth in the home of her youth. Grand-mother was alive and comfortable, if not healthy. Gailin also sensed someone else, large and moving, almost shouldering her thoughts aside as he paced back and forth but she didn't dare investigate. She would meet him soon enough.

"She's there," Gailin told her protector. "Wish me luck," she added as her hand reached out for the cabin door.

Chapter 4

Back Home

Overall her cabin looked just as it had the night the villagers had come to arrest her. The wood in the fire box had been replenished but other than that, it was the same. Grandma nestled in her blankets didn't stir when Gailin closed the door and looked about her with wonder. The sorcerer who stood on the far side of the table looked at her without surprise and wordlessly motioned for her to go see how her grandmother fared. As if Gailin's return were a common occurrence, he began to ladle out two bowls of the stew she had detected. She couldn't resist, but went to kneel at grandmother's side and found her little changed. Her thin, soft skin looked so pale Gailin could almost see through to the veins that ran beneath. Gently Gailin rested her hand against grandma's cheek and whispered, "I'm here."

Her grandmother didn't react, though Gailin's face passed through the dreams behind the dimmed eyes.

For her part the younger woman rose unsteadily to her feet and now addressed herself to the other occupant of the single room cabin. The sorcerer was tall and lean, dark featured and very angular, making it hard to determine his age. His neatly trimmed hair and beard bespoke of time and money, but not a single silver hair to speak of age. His finely cut suit and boots seemed out of place in a simple cabin like this. A dark navy cloak of velvet rested over one of the chairs as if he had only just arrived and she wondered how he would explain himself.

Trying mightily to keep her voice steady, Gailin addressed him as he finished setting the table. "Thank you, sir, for watching over her. Who are you?"

"I was in town, passing through and heard about a lady having to abandon her grandmother because of a rather remarkable hanging and thought I could help. Jonis was here but asked me to watch so he could get back to his crops. I hope you're hungry. I'm not much of a cook."

Gailin steadied her shields before she thought about Jonis with a pit of fear drilling through her. She knew instinctively that her friend would have stayed here, not passed this duty off on another, especially a stranger. What had happened to Jonis? She dare not think about her fear for the poor farmer. Instead she put her hand into her pockets and felt the Heart Stone there and it gave her strength to move on.

"I am hungry, sir, but you didn't answer my question. Who are you?"

The tone of her voice must have said something to him, for he paused before he pulled out the chair for her. "Come, sit Gailin. I'm Drake."

With her hand on the Heart Stone Gailin saw a flash of change in the sorcerer's appearance. Because of the name magic demanding her to come take a seat, she had to obey, but not without a fearful glance at the snake's tongue that slithered out of his mouth when he said his name. He was a liar at best and the Heart Stone made that visible. Was it a truth detector? Perhaps, but she expected she would see far more if she could somehow make his true nature visible. Now was not the time for her to challenge him. Instead she deliberately walked past the proffered chair and took the one opposite.

"It looks wonderful, and I am hungry," she admitted, not making eye contact with the gentleman but instead looked at the venison stew and crusty bread he had prepared. Had he made this magically or was he skilled at cooking?

Unfazed by her rejection of his polite manners, Drake sat at the seat he had pulled out and they began eating. Gailin, for her part, kept her hand off the Heart Stone. She didn't want the magic or her reaction to what it showed her to give her away. She disbelieved all of what Drake told her as he explained how he had come to be in her home. However, when he mentioned that he knew better how to tend to the diseases and conditions of aged people, this fired her interest.

"You are a healer?" she asked.

"After a fashion," he admitted. "I've studied the human body and many of the diseases found in other lands and thought I could share them here."

Gailin had to stop eating just to stare at Drake. Vamilion had warned her that this sorcerer would seem kinder than he actually was, but she hadn't believed Drake would be so charming and have the same skills as her. She must not let down her guard, but she was indeed fascinated. "How did you know I was interested in healing?"

Drake didn't admit anything at first, but he focused on her intently. "I heard about you in the village. Everyone begged me to stay since you had run off and there was no one to act as a healer. I think they regret ever distrusting you," he murmured and his dark green eyes gleamed invitingly.

Behind her shield Gailin had to remind herself that she had been pulled here against her will. She was his slave. She must not be lured by his enchantments. He was a deceiver, no matter how mannerly or gentle he might seem. She must make him only believe that she was interested in what he had to offer.

"Can you teach me?" she whispered.

Drake cocked his head slightly, as if surprised. "I probably know less about healing than you. The body, I know, but not the herbs and medicines, nor the methods that might work."

Gailin swallowed her fear and went on the offensive. "Then a sharing of knowledge," she proposed. "I will teach you of the medicines I know if you will teach me how the body works. Perhaps that way we can both grow in our understanding." This suggestion came abruptly, boldly, brushing away her fear of it. This must be a Wise One's prompting. Somewhere privately she remembered that Vamilion wanted her to learn magic from this dark practitioner and this would do it. She would learn more than magic from him and make him pay for ever manipulating her.

* * *

Vamilion stood frozen on the edge of the forest in utter terror. He didn't know how to act and the Wise One instincts at first provided no guidance. He easily recognized the menacing presence of this sorcerer who had stalked him for years. The hunted had watched his hunter for some time and knew the evil of which Drake was capable. Vamilion's fear came from that understanding and while he had tried to warn Gailin, it would have been impossible to prepare her by giving her that knowledge. Better to arm her than warn her, he told himself. But that didn't comfort him as he stood helpless, staring blindly into the darkness, unable to see the cabin that his magical senses told him sheltered just beyond in the trees.

How could he help her? Vamilion used magic to listen in on the conversation and approved how Gailin's shield over her thoughts remained steady, but that also meant he had no idea what she was planning. He didn't want to get close enough to understand her. Could he get past the sorcerer's own shields and snap that neck with a well-placed magical blow before Drake knew of the attack? Again

Vamilion had to battle with the completely ridiculous idea of letting her perish, allowing him to go home to Paget, content in the knowledge that he would one day find another Gailin, long after Paget had died and he would not be faced with this moral dilemma. Or would that even work now that he had given Gailin the Heart Stone? Probably not.

Of course it was an idle and evil thought, unworthy of a Wise One. He had sworn himself to help all the citizens of the Land, including Gailin. He had just put her into the viper's den and would immediately pull her back out if he could. Vamilion knew he would sacrifice himself rather than let a single strand of that brilliant warm hair be harmed. He remembered its stunning shade from when he had touched her braid, ever so briefly, as he placed that noose around her neck and now it remained burned into his mind. He wanted to study the color, like amber or a topaz in the deep wells of the mountains.

Stop it! Vamilion snarled at himself as he reined in his wandering mind and concentrated again. The grandmother was alive and asleep. Drake had no idea how much magic, if any, Gailin possessed and she seemed in no immediate danger. That left Vamilion safe to watch closely and craft a few ideas of how to kill Drake the instant Vamilion sensed his motivations turned and would be a threat to Gailin. How long until Drake gave up trying to puzzle out Gailin's powers and revealed his true self? Part of Vamilion wished it would not be long. He wanted her out of danger, off Seeking on her own. The patience of the mountain within him only built up the tension until it snapped in an earthquake; hopefully one that could bury Drake forever, despite his interminably long life.

While he waited, to distract himself, Vamilion crafted a letter to Paget, carving it into his tablet rather than using ink or graphite. He had set up this system years ago so that she would see a corresponding tablet in their home in the mountains and know he was thinking of her. It was not unlike the book he had given Gailin, but the act of carving his little notes to his wife was more to his liking, comforting even. He chiseled his message and then blew away the chips and stone dust to read what he'd crafted.

"I'm in the forest, far from you. It will be a while longer. I am finally going to challenge the snake. Sleep well, my love."

After he finished, he wrote some commentary in Gailin's book, giving her his thoughts on what Drake had revealed in the evening's conversation, but he didn't put the compulsion on it, only giving her the desire to look when it was a safe time. That could wait. Nothing urgent. But as he set aside his stylus, Vamilion shuddered. It felt wrong to write to both women in such a similar, intimate way. Was he already being unfaithful? His message to Paget was only of love, while the words to Gailin would keep her alive. He didn't want to see the similarities, but they were there, waiting to come out in the light of day and he knew it. Vamilion sat in this virtual cavern of avoidance, choosing not to come out even though he knew the passageway was right before him. He would rather wait in his dark isolation a bit longer, under the crushing mountain of indecision a few more years.

Resolutely, he decided to think of his own comfort and conjured himself a camp since he probably would be there on the forest edge for a time. Fire, tent, and a warm meal appeared while he listened to Gailin's conversation with Drake. Part of him wanted to be jealous of the charm the magician was implementing, but Vamilion also wanted to resist it. Gailin had a right to be courted by any man she chose. However, the Mountain King also yearned nothing more than to burst in on them and warn her, preferably while throttling the lying demon, that everything he was saying was an evil seduction. Another part of him hoped that she was seeing through his deceptions for herself. Vamilion couldn't tell without going into her mind and he almost swore himself into not doing anything, at least until he was free to love her. However, an oath by a Wise One was binding, so he didn't dare.

* * *

Gailin felt terribly tired after her long day but also too afraid to close her eyes. Could she dare sleep with this man in her house? Could she keep her shields up even in her dreams? What about the awkwardness of sleeping arrangements? There were only the two small beds and Grandmother already occupied one.

"So, where do you live?" she asked conversation-ally, trying to bring up the uncomfortable topic as she washed up the dishes and Drake banked the fire.

"Anywhere you want me to," he replied, not look-ing back at her, but his voice had changed, turning even more matter-of-fact. Abruptly Gailin realized he had not answered her question, but instead made it a proposition. This could be dangerous for her in more ways than one. Was he trying to seduce her? When he could have just commanded her? Perhaps he wanted to have her come to him willingly. The thought had not occurred to her, for she had been so concerned about the magic. She had not considered what he might want to do to her body. She had never imagined herself a beauty or that someone would want her that way. Even Jonis had held back, uncer-tain and awkward, after he realized how busy she was with her healing.

Just as she felt she might panic at these terrible considerations, an inspired Wise One idea emerged. "I think there are extra blankets in the attic. I can get them for you and we will make you a bed." At the same moment she was creating the blankets so it wasn't a lie until she knew if she had been successful or not. It was subtle magic that he hopefully would not notice. Instead she went to the ladder that led up into the rafters to the attic – really a few planks placed across the ceiling joists – and found what she had created and then tossed down to him.

Why was she accepting his invasion of her life? If she truly had just returned home, unaware of the name magic, Drake should be on his way. Wouldn't that be how it would be if she found Jonis here waiting for her, watching over Grandmother? Perhaps not this late, but he would definitely be heading home in the morning. So why was she expecting Drake to stay? Was it because she knew he held her name over her head, because he had offered the lure of medical training, or was she attracted to him?

More questions than she could count, let alone concentrate upon. Witlessly she blew out the lantern and lay down fully dressed in her bed, letting Drake make his own way with the blankets. She wasn't being a courteous hostess but at the moment, she really didn't care. Gailin wished privately that she had the energy to open up her book and write a bit, but it could wait until morning. Since her grandmother had fallen ill, Gailin had developed an internal clock, allowing her to waken at whatever time she must to tend to Grandmother's needs, and she did so now. She wanted to wake an hour before dawn so that she may go out and write to Vamilion without observation. Hopefully she would feel better, safer in the morning light, with a dangerous stranger on the other side of the room from her.

Much to her surprise, she did sleep and dream.

The dream came as an unexpected shift from her fear. For one thing, Grandma guided her on the way, wandering through twisting, spongy tunnels that pulsed with a squishing beat. The disgusting surroundings didn't seem to faze Grandma, who took her hand, cheerful and chattering, healthy and whole again, as she had been in Gailin's oldest recollections. "Memory and knowledge are on the outer sides, vision in the very back and while these would be good, let's go down some levels and see where the emotions are. It could take ages to get to where he truly resides. It's his feelings we must seek."

"What do you mean, Grandma?" Gailin asked, pulling back against her guide's firm grip. Indeed it felt like she was a child again, being dragged from her parent's funeral after the plague had taken them and now she must go, willing or no, with her Grandmother. She wanted to remain behind, but that was not an option and now these sticky, oozing passageways must be navigated. Where was Grandma taking her?

"You'll want to see this. There are the souls you must free," Grandma insisted as they ducked down deeper and the passages grew darker; a sickly purple red and the floor over which they stepped grew slick with the moisture that seeped off the surface. Meanwhile the throbbing that seemed to echo through the paths grew louder, more insistent. Gailin thought it familiar but when she realized it was a heartbeat, she pulled back again mightily.

"Grandma, are we inside someone?"

The elder woman looked back at her as if this was obvious. "The mind of a murderer, a Soul Eater. You must seek for the light and snuff it out. Find the fire within and douse it. And his resides in the lower places. Where it is dark and warm. He has kept them there, trapped and has fed off them."

"Them?" Gailin asked with a chilled thought. She suspected where she had been transported but she dare not think it, let alone say it aloud even in her dreams.

"The Eaten Ones," Grandma insisted and then pulled her back into moving down through the brain of a demon, past Drake's memories and into the cortex where emotions dwelt. The fascinated healer of Gailin's personality wondered at the pulsing and texture of the material about them. How did it store information, process life and encase a soul? She wanted to reach out and touch, but the wiser part of her knew that would be dangerous. She was within an evil brain within a dream. There would be better places to study and learn.

Grandma had at last brought her to the destination she sought, down at the base of the skull, almost black with blood and the dark of Drake's thoughts. Gailin wanted, and yet dare not try to see better, or call up some light. She could barely make out the wall of a membrane before her. It was ribbed, but thin as gauze and translucent. Encased in the sac of tissue that filled the passageway, she saw faces and hands pressed against the barrier, straining against it, stretching out the material. She could almost imagine their screams, for she could see their mouths, open in horror, pressed, breathless and struggling to be free. She coiled back in terror.

"The souls he feeds on," Grandma confirmed. "Remember and do not be deceived."

Chapter 5

Lessons in Hard Things

Gailin burst awake gasping. Her eyes saw nothing, for dawn had not yet lifted. She struggled to control her breathing and oriented herself. Greatly daring, she reached her mind out to brush against Grandmother, and found she too was just coming out of a dream but she would not waken for a while. The poor old woman slept more than anything nowadays, which was probably for the best. If she knew what the granddaughter she had raised was going through Grandmother would die of fright right there.

Next Gailin reached very carefully toward the front of the room where she had heard Drake make his bed the evening before. To her surprise, he was gone, or she could not sense him. She pushed out farther, seeking in the darkest hour of the night. With her magic she brushed against Vamilion's shields, sleeping a few miles beyond the river. She needed answers and she needed them now. Ruthlessly, she shook Vamilion awake with a jarring thought and then snatched up the book, realized she couldn't see to write and had to fumble with the lantern to get enough light while she listened to Vamilion's mind groggily come to awareness. By the time she knew he could concentrate, she had hastily scratched dozens of questions into a randomly opened page.

"He's not here. What should I do? He just assumed he could stay here and I'm frightened. He hasn't done anything overtly magical, but he spent the night and I was able to conjure blankets without him noticing but... but I think he wants more than magic from me. His tongue is split like a snake..."

Her hand froze and she realized what she'd done again. Vamilion had to stop her in order to get a word in edgewise.

"Relax, you're doing well," Vamilion wrote. "He suspects, but he does not know. You talked about medicine and apparently you've come to an agreement to teach each other. This is good. He left toward town soon after you fell asleep to get something, I suspect, for that teaching. He will be back soon. He won't leave you now that he's got you in his trap. You saw his forked tongue because the Heart Stone shows you the truth when you need to see it. If you put him fully under a spell of truth you would see a monster. Don't do that. It's unnecessary and he would know. So what have you learned about him that I couldn't hear in a conversation?"

"Does a dream count?" she wrote, having forgotten that in her panic at realizing Drake had gone. For all she knew the dream was a foreshadowing of him returning with a command for her to die.

"No, he values you. Tell me about your dream," Vamilion ordered.

Slowly she set out for Vamilion all she had experienced in Drake's brain during the tour led by her grandmother. Though the imagery haunted, she had no problem interpreting it. "You are right," Vamilion declared as she finally stopped writing. "This confirms that he is a Soul Eater. He uses the lives of his victims to keep his going. We will have to release all of the souls before he can actually be killed. It's a good thing I did not challenge him or you would be dead. Now, other than in his brain, did you gain any understanding of where these souls are stored?"

"It's at the base of his brain. My grandmother made it a point to say it wasn't in his vision or knowledge areas or movement, or any of his senses, but down near the base, where emotions reside."

"It seems a study of anatomy is necessary on many levels then," Vamilion commented. "This is good. I had not learned that he was a Soul Eater. Has he shown you any magic at all?"

"Not unless you count making himself at home without me being offended. I don't know if I'm being seduced, bespelled or if I really want to learn what he's offering to teach me. All I know is that he's staying in my home and I can think of no safe way to kick him out."

"Then his goals and your Wise One instincts are on the same path, at least for the time being. Do you feel safe enough to go on your own for a bit. I want to speak to Owailion about this situation and I cannot persuade him to come from here. I must go north for a while."

"Can we still write?" she asked.

"Yes, the book will still reach me no matter how far the distance. I will come back as quickly as I can. I'm still Seeking an efficient means of magical travel. If Owailion would simply answer me when I call him I would not need to go to him at all."

Gailin stopped him with one more question. "Before you go, can you find my friend Jonis? He would have come to protect Grandmother while I was gone, and Drake said he went back to his farm, but I saw the tongue flick at that and I don't believe him."

He sensed no reluctance at this request, as if Vamilion would have done anything for her. "Where does this Jonis live? Can you show me a picture?" he asked.

Gailin hadn't tried this magical skill before, but she concentrated, imagining Jonis' apple farm set half a mile south down the river from the village where the young man had homesteaded by planting a struggling orchard. The apples were the only thing that distinguished it from all the other hardscrabble homes in the area. Then Gailin imagined herself bundling that image into a folded page and passed that impression toward the book where it made an imprint of her vivid detail right on the page.

"I've got it. That was good work. You should add pictures of your plants that way. It's better than drawing," Vamilion commented. "I will return as soon as I can."

Gailin felt Vamilion's mind fading as he departed into the dawn that began dusting the window outside. She didn't dare go back to sleep right now, but thought longingly of a bath while Drake was not here. Resolutely she rose and went to get the water bucket. Usually she bathed in the river if it was warm enough and she would use magic right now to warm the water a bit rather than wash in the cabin in case Drake were to return. Grandma would sleep a while longer.

By the time she got back, having also washed her shift, Drake had returned with a strange load that he had heaved onto the table, wrapped in canvas.

"Good morning," he said without comment at her absence.

Fearfully she murmured the same. Since he did not begin to explain his huge package, Gailin began her own project for the morning. She carefully poured a measured amount of water into her pot. Then, as she began adding the various ingredients for her healing broth, she also started instructing. "I add cayenne for arthritis, cinnamon for the heart."

"Is this all written in your book?" Drake asked as he watched her pulling powders out of the larder.

"They will be. I've not had a chance to write much yet. I will put the drawings of the plants as well as how to prepare the ingredients and their uses. It's best to memorize this, for few can read here in the Land."

"So I've noticed. How is it that you learned?" Drake asked with little sincere curiosity.

Gailin recognized that he only wanted to know more about her to manipulate her, so she kept her instructions interspersed, making it seem less intimate to have him know so much about her that was harmless. "Cloves for inflammation," she added and then looked over at Grandma. "She taught me. She's from Malornia, where they learned to read, but could do little else because of the magic. She taught me all I know."

"You must care for her," Drake commented, looking at the labels on the bottles rather than at the woman who had provided the knowledge. "How old is she?"

Gailin shuddered with a hidden fear now. Would he swallow Grandma and add her to his collection of souls in the bottom of his brain? "I have no idea," she replied flatly. "Now, coriander seeds are good for bowels and relaxing her nerves but the cilantro it grows works better. It's too early in the season for the plant. Next add garlic for the stomach and general infections."

"I'd prefer to read these instructions, but I can't," Drake said frankly.

"You can't read?" Gailin looked over at him with surprise. Given his suave manner and rich bearing she had just assumed he had the leisure time to learn the much valued skill.

"I cannot read the language of the Land," he qualified. "No one understands this, but there's a spell here. Only those who live here and intend to never leave can actually speak the language. Did it never occur to you that your grandmother never spoke Malornian with you? When she came here she intended to stay and so she became part of the spell. She taught you to write in the new language because that is what the spell demanded. Those of us who do not intend to stay, while we can perhaps learn your language, we have to be taught it like a foreign language, and there are so few who can teach it. I've only been here a few years and always have wanted to return to my home, so while I can speak the language, it's nearly impossible to learn to read it."

Gailin's hands stilled in the stirring of her additives to the broth. Was he subtly asking to be taught to read? If so, she was not going to acquiesce until he used name magic on her to demand it. Instead she redirected the conversation back at him. "Where are you from?" then added, "Ginger, for digestion."

"Malornia, like your grandmother. I came to see why everyone wanted to come here but I also came to set up trade routes, though it's difficult. I understand why people come and stay."

Rather than accept the compliment to her homeland Gailin added more to her broth. "Mustard seed for tumors and if you grind it, the paste is excellent for skin sores. So why do people come and want to stay?" she continued.

Drake shrugged, trying and failing to be nonchalant about the question. "There's almost no magic used here. Many people immigrated for freedom from magic. The Land is beautiful and the weather is varied. You can find almost anything to your taste. It grows crops well and while it is too newly opened to know its true resources, the Land can at least feed its people. But it will be years before you are ready for the trade I offer."

"Nutmeg for dementia and infections," Gailin continued. "What do you offer in trade?"

Drake smelled the concoction and curled up his nose in disgust. "Knowledge for the most part. I know who to do business with if you want silk, gold, copper, bronze, gems, lumber, leather, and iron, almost anything. And I know how to make deals. I know what goes into the 'broth' of a business. Is there more to go into this broth?"

"Yes, I add sage, to keep her calm and her mind safe and turmeric, for cancers and to increase her appetite overall. Finally I add milk and honey so it tastes better, though the combination isn't tasty in the least. Milk and honey also add just about every nutrient a human needs."

Drake helped her lug the pot over to the fire and then asked, "And you grow all these things for yourself?"

"Most of them," Gailin commented. "Some of them don't grow in this soil so I had to put them in pots – cinnamon, turmeric and nutmeg are all tropical, but the rest can be grown here if I'm careful. We're farther south than it seems here, but there is plenty of water so it doesn't get so dry. The bees love it here."

They worked over the broth until it was almost warm and then Gailin woke Grandma to feed her the gruel and then gave her a washcloth bath, rolling her so that she did not develop bed sores. "She would still get up and go with me for a walk until this last winter. Now she doesn't have the strength. I'm afraid I'm losing her," Gailin admitted sadly after she laid the withered woman back down and covered her shoulders with the thick blankets again.

"I'm sorry," Drake replied grimly, but his tongue flashed reptilian and Gailin remembered. Although they had spent a comfortable hour and she had learned much from him, she still was a captive to his evil. Now with her chores finished Gailin looked over at the canvas bag that occupied the entire sizable table in the middle of the one room cabin, hoping to change the subject.

"Oh, I thought I should bring something so that I may pay for my half of the education. You wanted to study anatomy and the only place I could easily get a body was in the village's ice house; your fellow criminals have not been buried yet."

In horror Gailin looked at Drake and then at the canvas package. He had brought a hanging victim here?

"They were keeping it in the ice house until they decided what to do with him. It's the murderer, not the rapist," Drake said as if this would make it any better. When he saw the look on her face he continued to try to justify his actions. "Well, no one else was going to deal with him and we have the need. Where else are we going to find a body to study?"

"How...how...how do people in other lands study medicine?" she managed to ask.

Drake looked almost amused at her uneasiness as he replied. "Same, only there the convicts know this will be their fate. If there is no family to protest, then their body will be used to help save other people. Since he killed his wife and there were no children, I thought this was fitting," and Drake threw back the canvas covering like he was opening a present, expecting her to be pleased.

Despite being stored in the coolest place in the village, decay had set in and the wave of putrid air made Gailin gag. Gray spots popped up on the corpse's already pasty skin and the back of his neck and hands had turned a nasty purplish gray color. His eyes, open and glazed to a milky haze looked particularly startled. Gailin put her hand over her nose and approached the table. Something in her was fascinated by this process and although the source appalled her, she was willing to learn from it.

And learn, she did. They spent the entire day cutting away different parts of the cadaver with the excellent knives that Drake just happened to have. Gailin took copious notes and made drawings in her book while they worked. They argued the function of the less familiar parts they found in the gut, some so mysterious they could only be speculated at. The liver, stomach and intestines were well known, but other pieces were set aside in whatever containers Gailin could find in her potting shed. Then they skinned the poor man to study his musculature. The tendons and ligaments fascinated her, for she could identify why the man walked with a limp, as she recognized him from town.

Drake, for his part seemed unusually preoccupied with the eyes and neck, like these carried more significance than other parts. He studied the neck muscles and trachea with morbid fascination, opening the vocal box to actually study its construction although it had been crushed by the actual hanging. He also plucked the eye out of the socket and shaved thin slivers off the iris to look at later. It made Gailin's empty stomach heave, but then what she was doing would not make anyone comfortable. Indeed, neither suggested that they would eat that day; not with the cooking surface occupied by a cadaver and their hands covered in every bodily fluid known.

By unspoken accord they agreed to stop as the light got dim, before launching into stripping away the muscle to reveal the bones for their next series of studies. The smell was only growing worse and when Gailin suggested boiling the body to get rid of the flesh, Drake reminded her that the brain would be lost. That made her pause. She wanted to study the brain most of all, even above the heart which was sitting in vinegar in her potting shed. In the end, they cut off the head and put it in a bucket of vinegar and then used her huge soap making pot to boil the body overnight so they could reassemble the skeleton in the morning. For her own part, Gailin went at twilight and took another bath at the river just to get the gore off and to somehow come to terms with what she had done.

Over the next few days she ate little and slept exhausted enough to ease the nightmares that such work might have induced. This did not soothe her conscious of the guilt she felt at studying with Drake, but she was learning. Something in her yearned to know how everything worked and she didn't want to stop until she understood. She used the evenings to draw her observations and utilized magic to make her drawings more detailed, above her poor ability to actually recreate her vision. And devotedly she wrote to Vamilion in the back of the pages where it would fade almost immediately, hopefully read nonetheless. She didn't hear much from him and her curiosity over his activities tickled her mind. What was he going to ask Owailion? She had little to say about Drake and how they would break him but someday she knew they would. She hoped they could kill him. There rested her entire hope for survival.

Chapter 6

Owailion

Vamilion looked out over the plain with a bleak eye. The flat stark landscape blanketed with heather and moss as far as his eye could see, pink and yellow, white and lavender with the occasional effort at green held little attraction to him. He much preferred the great black volcano behind him. Jonjonel had not erupted in several years and his sense was it would be four or more years yet, before he would get to witness that spectacle again. On the very edge of the continent, isolated and by far the largest mountain in the Land, the temperamental, yet predictable volcano provided the best backdrop for this meeting. Besides, it was halfway for Owailion and him to meet.

Getting the equally temperamental Wise One to talk with him always seemed less about compromise and more about endurance. For Vamilion, he either had to make himself sick for hours after an instant trip, or he had to walk four days towards the nearest mountain. He elected to walk north west of Gailin's village and then use the like-to-like part of his magic to draw him from one peak to another to arrive at the base of Jonjonel. In all, four days to cross three thousand miles. For Owailion, it would be an instant trip from his home near the northern edge of the continent where ice remained almost year round. Owailion's magical means of travel left little to be desired: wish it and he was there.

The problem was in getting him to wish to come.

It took the patience of mountains to endure Owailion's attitude and rancor. The bitterness arrived before the customary pop of the magic that announced the King of Creating's arrival. Owailion's white head was bowed against the open wind and his bleak black eyes took in none of the scenery as he glared against the low sun that couldn't quite manage to completely set this time of year even though it was quite late in the evening. He looked older than his energy witnessed, for he could have run miles with ease, but his chronological age, along with everything else about Owailion's past remained buried. Owailion wasn't willing to talk about those times.

"Thank you for coming," Vamilion said in greeting.

"You didn't give me a choice," grumbled Owailion. "It was getting down-right loud."

Vamilion almost smiled at that. He had been magically requesting, calling at obnoxious hours and pestering for this interview every step of his travel here and not been nice about his demands. His mentor would complain about anything that got him away from his work, but Owailion also would be more than interested in anything that occurred in the Land, especially if it had to do with new Wise Ones. It still remained unclear how he knew about any of the magical happenings in the Land. Owailion rarely bothered to leave his home in the far north now that he had built all the palaces and hid the Talismans. Mostly he only roused himself when there might be an invasion, leaving Vamilion to do the lion's share of guarding the borders.

"Well, I found her and I thought you would want to know. And I need your help," Vamilion began.

"Help? With what? As I taught you, you can teach her," Owailion growled.

"It's not that simple. That hunter that has been stalking me? Well, he saw me find her and knows her name. I haven't challenged him yet because I'm not sure I can cut him off before he kills her with a word. Right now she's 'disguised' magically and I don't think the hunter knows exactly what he's lured, but he used name magic to bring her away from me. I need a decisive way to get past the sorcerer's shields and kill him without him even knowing I'm in the battle. If he's a Soul Eater, we must release the spirits he has consumed even before we can kill him. Then there's the family she is responsible for and....and I still have Paget. I won't let...let the new Queen see me until I have found ....until Paget has passed..."

As he said these words, Vamilion's appearance changed dramatically. Instead of simple leathers suitable for traveling and tramping across mountains and plains, he took on a regal appearance. He wore a blood wine colored jerkin of velvet quilted in gold stitching over a fine white silk shirt. His rugged pants were replaced with polished gray leather tooled with the outline of the mountain range just visible on the southern horizon behind them. Even his boots took on a polished sheen. Over it all he wore a luxuriously fur-trimmed and hooded cloak dyed a granite shade. Slung over his shoulder he carried a baldric that boasted platinum tooling from which hung a steel sword worthy of a king and a matching pick designed for both climbing as well as a handy weapon. This abrupt change in appearance did not surprise either man but Owailion looked at his companion and shook his head in disgust.

"You've still not learned to not make an oath, boy," Owailion muttered.

Patiently Vamilion replied, "Not when it comes to Paget. I made this oath years ago and I've not changed my mind. And I'm not a boy."

"You are a boy if you're foolishly still clinging to that old relationship. Hasn't finding your Queen changed your outlook?" asked Owailion. "Surely you can see that she's a much better fit for you than someone who is not magical and growing old and will die…"

Vamilion cut off his mentor, and with his denial his regal clothing just as abruptly turned back to his more customary attire. "I don't want to argue this with you again, Owailion. I haven't actually looked at …at the new Queen. From her skills and inclinations I'm thinking she's going to be a healer. Queen of Healing. It's different...more like your gifts. She's driven to study things rather than drawn to something in nature. As I was saying, she's in disguise. The hunter knows her name and used name magic to force her back to her home where she's tending her grandmother. He suspects she's magic but doesn't know her as a Wise One."

"How is it that you haven't looked at her if you gave her the Heart Stone?" Owailion asked, only slightly curious.

So Vamilion had to tell his mentor the entire story, including how he was now communicating with Gailin, though he stubbornly refused to utilize her name. Indeed they managed to simply call her the Queen or the Queen of Healing and left it at that.

"You're a fool," Owailion muttered after he heard all that Vamilion had tried to do and still planned. "She's going to die the instant that sorcerer figures out what he has there. And having the magician train her in mind work? Not a wise move in my opinion."

Vamilion swallowed his own frustration, plunging it into the stone pit of his mind and then as carefully as he could, replied, "What would you have done in my place?"

"I would have looked the girl in the eye and countered every command the sorcerer gave her with a command of my own. At least then she wouldn't be in the lair of a demon. She cannot hope to be hidden there forever, especially if she's studying medicine and magic with him."

Vamilion snapped back, "And when she didn't come to his demands, the sorcerer would know I was protecting her and kill her and I'd watch someone die in my arms all the sooner." Vamilion didn't want to point that out, but he knew eventually that seemed to be his fate; women he loved dying, slipping away despite all the magic he could bring to bear.

Owailion sighed in irritation before reluctantly nodding agreement.

"So we both agree I can't save her just by looking her in the eye and setting our bond," Vamilion continued. "But what do you think we should do to get her out of the sorcerer's grasp?"

Owailion might not like it, but sour looks were not a solution either. So Owailion had to propose another option and Vamilion listened carefully as his mentor's proposed his plan. "We need to drive the hunter into revealing his magic first. The Queen must ask more questions, getting him to teach her about himself, until he admits that he has magic. That will open the door to letting her into his head. She's already exploring how he's managed to stay alive for so long: he's a Soul Eater. She will have to release all the spirits he's absorbed before we can ever get near to killing him, and he cannot know that we're doing it until it's too late."

Vamilion shook his head rejecting the possibility before Owailion even finished his explanation. "I doubt we can release the souls without his noticing. He'll feel weakened and lash out to kill her if he thinks she's doing this, and then come after me if he suspects it's my doing."

"Not if he gets his energy from somewhere else," Owailion countered. "He's been absorbing from her for days now, hasn't he? The Soul Eater has not gone hunting since she came to him. You've been watching and tracking his movements. We know he has to feed daily and yet he hasn't left her side. He's not even tapped into the grandmother. He's feeding off the Queen's magical energy. We need to lure him into complacency, dependent on her presence and get them away from everyone else that might become his victim. He'll want to stay near her, keeping her alive so he can tap into her and her alone. Meanwhile we slowly release the souls he's absorbed."

"Won't that clue him in that he's got a Wise One?" Vamilion observed logically.

"Yes, but she's a Wise One on a leash," Owailion qualified. "He will love that he controls her. And if he controls her, then he controls you....even if you are not yet bonded. I am the only one on whom he has not got a grasp. I am free to act. I will drive them away from populated areas and watch over her. I'll lure them away where he cannot reach the ley lines and then we'll have out the battle, strip him down to his own bare life and by that time she will have found a way past his shields."

"Do you have a place to drive him in mind?" Accordingly Vamilion conjured a large scroll of map and a simple wooden table into being and unrolled the parchment to survey it. Unlike maps of other places, the Land had so few settlements no one bothered to mark the human habitations on this one. Instead this loose sketch, mostly Vamilion's exploratory work in the mountains showed three things: geological forms, bodies of water and ley lines. The lines where magic arched all across the Land, spread like hoarfrost over the geographic features.

Owailion peered at it. "Where did you find your Queen?"

"In a village here, on the edge of the Demion forest on the west side of the river where it meets the plains. Halfway between the Vamilion mountains and the Great Chain. Inconvenient, that," he muttered as he put his finger on the spot midway between the two mountain ranges on the Don River.

"And this is what attracted him in the first place." Owailion traced the green line that arched across the map without regards to the geographic features. The magic in these rivers of power must have been attractive to Outlander sorcerers like Soul Eaters who must tap into the power that way. Indeed it lured sorcerers and demons alike to the Land, which held more than its share of untapped magic and the ley lines spread like faults in the surface where the magic welled up to tempt them. "Where should we drive him if we're going to cut him off from the ley lines?"

"Toward the plains I suppose, though I won't be able to move ahead of them," and Vamilion slid his finger northwest out into the open spaces between the two rivers where the ley lines petered out.

"Or up into the mountains west of the lake no one has named," Owailion moved Vamilion's finger farther to the northwest. "This is where we'll have control."

"That's a long way," Vamilion commented, trying to not think of the thousand mile journey he was proposing. "You'll be the only one who can protect her. I can't go that far from the mountains."

"Both have their advantages: we get him so far away from the coast so he won't have a quick escape or access to ley lines. One of the reasons I was willing to come to meet you here is what I've foreseen approaching. Your Soul Eater is just the first in a series of waves. There's a second push of ships in a few weeks, sailing from the west and then a third coming overland from the southeast. They'll be here in a few months and we need to be ready. It would be nice to have a third magician up and trained when they come."

Vamilion straightened up from the map and arched his back, as if this news had stiffened him to stone. He wondered again how Owailion could be aware of these things beyond the Land. It was the one skill his mentor refused to teach him and he wondered if the King of Creating thought him incapable of seeing from afar.

Instead of worrying over that trivial problem, Vamilion focused on the immediate need. "Where will the ships land?" he asked as he dealt with a rising sense of panic. He wouldn't be able to help Owailion face magical invaders and still keep his distance from

Gailin over these two new threats. It wouldn't be possible, but he was sworn both ways: protect the Land and protect her.

Owailion just shrugged. "No idea. I'm keeping an eye on them and it seems the ships are coming from Malornia, and the overland wave is from Marewn and Demonia together. These waves are coming so fast they must be in collusion. And your hunter is at the heart of it. I suspect he's their forward scout."

Vamilion took a steadying breath. "Well, it cannot be helped. Let's see if we can kill the soul-eater first and train the queen before we have to confront a full invasion. I just wish there wasn't so much open and tempting land here that they want."

"It's not the Land, boy, it's the magic. Outlanders see how we use the magic and assume they can tap into what we have. They're wrong, but you cannot convince them of that. They will always want what they cannot have."

Chapter 7

Strategizing

Gailin looked through the book with wonder. In a matter of a few weeks she had written more on the human body than she thought she would learn in a lifetime. She had filled nearly half the book with detailed drawings of the body they had dissected. Also she took the time to actually write out a page for each of her favorite herbs and included drawings of the plants, seeds and combinations that seemed to work best. Gailin felt much healing detail still eluded her, but with all this work in one secure place, ready to access, she had never felt more empowered to help heal others.

However, when she applied what she had learned to her ailing grandmother, she immediately felt helpless again. The old woman continued to fade. Her brain seemed to drift, blending dreams with wakeful understanding. When she was conscious, Grandma seemed to think Gailin was a little girl again and would chastise her about keeping her hair tamed, or her hands clean. When Grandma caught sight of Drake about the house she became agitated, grumbling about strange men stealing from them.

Drake didn't comment on these accusations. Indeed, he seemed unfazed by anything that happened as they worked. He was tolerant of Gailin's need to tend the garden or when she asked him to run to the village for something since she dare not yet set foot there, lest she be recognized and the witch hunt begin again. Drake willingly slept on the floor, brought in wood, lugged water and put up with her experimental cooking. However, Gailin's suspicions remained hovering and she rarely wrote in her book when he was about, especially when she was writing to Vamilion. She wanted to practice her magic as much as her medicine but she still dare not attempt anything toward invading his mind. The thought chilled her.

Then, two weeks after Vamilion had left her, Gailin felt a prompting to look at the book. No name magic drove her to do this, heedless of her captor nearby, so she waited until Drake had gone to town to trade her harvested beans and berries for more of her healing spices. Then she snatched up the book to read Vamilion's message in the back of her precious messages.

"How do you fare?" was all he had written but she could have wept for the caring, for nothing so gentle or concerned came from Drake to ease her mind.

"Well enough," she wrote back. "Is there any word of Jonis?" She didn't want to admit it, but she missed the interaction with her farmer friend, or anyone for that matter. Working with Drake almost sucked the enjoyment of talking out of the room. He was so unemotional, almost cold and his personality only served to remind her that he was a sorcerer, unable to love anyone but himself.

"I'm afraid no one has seen him. I went to his farmhouse that you showed me and it appears abandoned. He didn't finish his pruning and that should have been completed weeks ago. I'm sorry to say he's probably a victim of this Drake, though we'll never be able to prove it."

Gailin tried not to cry, but she probably knew this already and hadn't wanted to admit it to herself. She didn't write her next comment immediately and when she did, she changed the subject completely. "I've learned a great deal about healing and ... and I think I can heal with my touch now. My grandmother's bed sores are almost instantly cured, the moment I find them. I don't think I'm actually curing her but it is magic and I don't have to concentrate on it so much as it just happens."

"That's how I am with stone," Vamilion's reply emerged with a strong stroke of his pen. "I just hold it in my hand and I know its makeup, where its flaws run and how to break it open. It is part of me being the King of the Mountains. And you are the Queen of Healing."

Gailin thought about that and the idea gave her a shiver of pleasure. She had already known her gift before she ever had touched the Heart Stone. Then she wrote further, "I assumed Wise One gifts were within nature, rivers and mountains and such."

"Not necessarily. Owailion's gift is to create machines and processes. He's a designer and a builder much like you are a healer. It's a fine gift. And speaking of Owailion, he's come to help us with Drake. Do not be surprised when the snake comes home and announces that you will have to leave soon. Owailion is going to be in the village asking questions, stirring suspicions. We want your sorcerer to feel nervous and want to leave. When he suggests this we want you to prompt him to head northwest, out onto the plains."

"Alright, but can I ask why?"

"I can try to explain. Magic energy is everywhere in the world. As Wise Ones we draw from the earth itself, which is why we really don't have limits on what we can do, short of the Heart Stone's moral limitations. However, other magicians out in the other countries cannot get their power from the earth. Some need to be possessed by demons which are basically evil versions of Wise Ones, able to tap into almost limitless magic inherently. Then there are other types of sorcerers who need to connect into ley lines. These are like rivers of magic where the power has come close to the surface and these magicians can perform their spells only when they are near one of these rivers. Drake is one of these. We hope that he will follow you and move away from the ley line he's been using here and become weaker because of it."

"Won't that make me weaker too?" Gailin asked.

"No, not in the least. Wise One power does not depend on ley lines. The only reason I'm even aware of them is because of my affinity to stone. Where the stone has borne a river of magic like a ley line, I can sense that and I have mapped those phenomena out of curiosity until I was able to tie these ley lines to where sorcerers had invaded the Land. They instinctively followed these lines to keep themselves magically charged. Drake will resist shifting away from them because he's moving into a void empty of them. He'll have to reveal his magic to move you back toward them or he'll go with you to the northwest away from them because he won't want to lose you."

"Lose me? He's practically my slave right now. He's fetching for me in the village as we speak."

"Yes, and that's another advantage of this. We cannot continue to risk him feeding on others. He's a Soul Eater. You saw that in your dream. He needs to absorb the souls of the dying...or ones he kills for himself in order to remain alive physically, just as he needs the ley lines to remain alive magically. Up until now he's done well enough without new souls because he's been with you. We don't want to stop that until you are far enough away from other people so that they aren't in danger of becoming his next meal."

This puzzled Gailin and she wrote, "How has he been surviving since he took me?"

"He's been feeding off you. It sounds awful, I know, but since you're a Wise One you are able to replenish without even noticing how you are tapped into the lifeblood of magic. Essentially you live forever because you are part of the magic of the world. And he's feeding on you."

Gailin shivered in horror, but she also inevitably felt her heartstrings tugging her toward something more important than her own life. "My grandmother?"

She could sense Vamilion's hesitancy about this touchy subject. He must already realize how much Gailin loved her only living relative and that would be a priority, even above saving her own life. Still, he did not hesitate to state what must be done. "She would be safer left behind. Would you trust one of us, Owailion or I to watch over her until....until this is finished? She will only be another target if you can talk Drake into leaving here and taking her with you."

For the longest time Gailin thought about her dilemma. She did not want her grandmother to end up as one of those horrible trapped souls she had witnessed in her tour of Drake's brain. However, neither could she feel good about leaving her grandmother behind. And physically her grandmother could never endure a trip anywhere, even in the gentlest wagon. Gailin also knew she was fighting a losing battle trying to keep her grandmother's flickering flame alight. Eventually the old woman would die, no matter how many healing and magical skills her granddaughter could acquire. Taking Drake away from here, leaving the old woman safe could be the best prospect for survival.

"Very well," she wrote regretfully. "But I want you to be the one to stay behind with her. You, I know…after a fashion and Owailion, I don't. From what you've told me, he's not a patient person…and you have to be to tend the dying."

"Then you've not been able to help her with your new gifts? I'm sorry. It is the way of nature and the Heart Stone will not allow you to interfere with it. You will find that sometimes there simply is no answer."

Gailin knew exactly what he meant before she wrote, "Like you and Paget?"

"In precisely the same way. My waiting is simply longer than yours. No, it's a good thing that I stay behind to watch over your grandmother. Owailion will be able to train you face to face once we have dealt with this Soul Eater. Tell him everything you learn about Drake, in your dreams and your other impressions. The answers will come to you more than to us."

"Then can I say, I don't think Drake has emotions. He has been here for days and never has initiated a conversation to get to know me or tried to be friendly. I am just another tool and this is not his home, just a laboratory to him. He has interests but he tries to keep them hidden from me: eyes, voices, necks, these fascinate him in a terrifying way. It is disturbing."

"Disturbing," Vamilion confirmed. "Now, how is your progress at getting past his shields? Has he suspected any magic from you?"

"Not that I've seen. I use so little: warming the creek when I bathe, magically putting my drawings in the book rather than doing so by hand. That reminds me; he cannot read our language. He said something about a spell, a language spell. If you do not intend to stay here in the Land, you may learn our language but you have to study it? Well, he has no intention of staying and so he cannot read our words. He said he was a trader; that he set up connections to make trade with other lands possible, but that the Land was too newly settled and that we had nothing to trade."

Gailin again garnered a sense of Vamilion's appreciation of this information, as if he were infusing words on the page with his pride in her work. "Interesting, I knew of the language spell. The Queen of River's doing before she died. It's subtle and few people who immigrate here realize they are speaking words they never technically learned. It's also an excellent way to recognize someone who is not coming to settle. Even if they study the language, their accent will give them away. Good, keep learning about him. Now, how should I treat your grandmother?"

Gailin chuckled to herself and then wrote carefully, "Not with any of the plants that you added to my book. You'll poison her and be up on charges of murder. I'll leave detailed instructions under her pillow when we leave. Speaking of which, how is Drake going to suggest we move? You said he would probably be willing to admit he's magic in order to leave quickly."

"That is the hope. Now....is he returning? I can feel him. Is he near?

Gailin closed the book without replying, threw the precious record unceremoniously on the bed and

went about fixing lunch as if she hadn't ignored all
the weeding she had intended to do that morning.
Her garden was really taking off and she needed to
stay ahead of it but if they would be leaving....well
that changed her plans and she wasn't going to worry
about it now. Instead she spread out her senses to
hear if her nemesis truly was returning.

Chapter 8

Confrontations

When he wanted to, Owailion could be downright scary. The wave of power he pushed up the river path and against the forest unnerved the animals and set the village babies crying before he even arrived in town. The disguise he chose, however, was anything but frightening. He came magically appearing as Jonis, dressed the way Gailin had remembered him, striding into town as if he hadn't been away for weeks. He deliberately hovered at the village market, buying vegetables and purchased an unworked leather skin to put them in and use later as if he might be patching his boots with it. The farmer's face was familiar to everyone and he returned many greetings, but didn't engage in any conversation. He wanted to be seen, to spook the Soul Eater. Had the dead arisen to accuse him? The question lingered in the summer air.

And Drake on his errand for the Queen of Healing obviously knew something was amiss. Owailion sensed him fluttering against his shields and then retreating. Drake might have caught a sneaking look from around a building corner and recognized the face of his murder victim. Owailion decided then to stroll toward the northern edge of town, walking for all the world like he wanted to go visit his friend Gailin. Drake must have fled like the hounds of hell nipped at his heels, for nothing else confronted Owailion's magic that washed like a sea wave over the area. Let the sorcerer get to the house and make his plans. Meanwhile Owailion, disguised as Jonis, sat in the summer shade of the forest along the pathway, ate his purchased lunch and began converting his leather into something useful, like a whip. Owailion always liked to have something at hand on which to work.

* * *

Even though she knew Drake was coming, Gailin jumped a little when the door slammed open. She almost dropped the pot she was carrying to the fire when he burst in and surprisingly said her name. "Gailin, we've got a problem."

She had at first expected panic from him, but then realized a man like Drake, with so few true emotions, would not feel fear or even urgency, no matter what prompted him to return so quickly. He still carried the beans she had sent with him and none of the spices she needed. Instantly she knew where his concern would focus and it came out of her mouth before she had a chance to think about it.

"They know I'm here?" she asked, letting herself feel the panic that would have engendered in her naturally.

"Yes," Drake said frankly, lying with his serpent's tongue. "We'll have to leave or they'll come get you again."

"We? You're offering to go with me? What about my grandmother?"

"We'll find someone to watch over her, but you must go now, before sunset. They're going to come for you and this time they'll burn you at the stake." Though Drake's words seemed frantic, his voice remained emotionless as he walked over to the clothing chest and began pulling things out of it. He gathered flint and steel, a frying pan, spoon and knife, making a pile in the middle of her bed while she stood there watching him, unable to move.

"How are we going to do this?" Gailin gasped, feeling true fear, not needing to play a role, for her emotion was genuine and the thought of being alone, tramping across the wilderness with this man who would and could kill her with a thought came from a real place. Then she managed to remember she promised to leave Vamilion directions and she fetched her book out of the pile of her belongings to carefully pull out a few precious pages and begin writing on them. "We've got nothing and nowhere to go?" she added to get Drake talking and to give her more time to write.

"Gailin, stop panicking," he ordered, and she felt the heavy fist of a compulsion descend on her. She stopped breathing for a moment and stared back up at him, unable to move. "Now, do you have something to carry these things in?" he asked tonelessly.

Carefully she looked him in the eye and said the truth. "No, I have nothing. What did you just do to me?"

This bald question, recognizing he had used name magic on her, finally got him to react a bit. "I asked you to stop panicking and you had to. I've ….it's a bit of magic I have. Like you. You've got a gift and so do I. We'll make a team of it. We'll be fine. Now, do you have any ideas how to carry all of this?"

Released from his magic-induced calm, Gailin managed to keep it for herself. She finished her notes, walked over to him beside the bed, plopped the book in the pile and scooped all her belongings into a tidy package in the blanket. When she didn't deny the magic, nor comment on it, he smiled subtly and turned toward the larder to gather food for their journey. He made a similar bundle of the blankets he had used since moving in with her and within minutes they were prepared to leave. She stood with her bundle at her feet, looking around the place and felt no fear. Was that from Drake's induced calm or was she really at ease with leaving her grandmother behind in Vamilion's hands and facing her first true adventure as a Wise One, in constant danger of being killed by her traveling companion? She couldn't tell.

Drake must have interpreted her daydreaming as something else and came to her, pulling her out of her reverie when he put his hand under her chin, making her look up at his deeply set eyes. "Don't worry, Gailin, I'll be with you and you'll be with me."

There was no compulsion in his words, but she steeled herself for it so when he unexpectedly leaned down and kissed her, she didn't react. While it shocked her, she didn't flinch. His lips felt cold and firm, hardly there for her, and she had to swallow her revulsion like bile. Kissing a wall? No, kissing a snake? She could just imagine that forked tongue and almost gagged suddenly. All her steadiness in carefully slicing a body into ribbons had not prepared her for the icy understanding that a monster was manipulating her and she still had no way out of it.

"Lean into him girl," a strange voice growled into her head. "Let him think he stands a chance. You'll be able to get behind his shields with that eventually."

Gailin obeyed the voice, though she didn't know who it was. Certainly Vamilion's gentle rumble would be recognized and welcomed, so this must be Owailion. She closed her eyes and leaned into the kiss, smiling against the cold embrace. Anything to escape Drake's mind hold over her. She could pretend. It wasn't a lie if she meant to kill him eventually. Instead she thought of how it would be to kiss another human and imagined it was Vamilion there holding her head against his, twining his fingers among the woven strands of her loose braid.

Thankfully Drake, emotionless as he was, didn't recognize her hesitation as more than surprise and seemed gratified that she had not rejected his awkward attempt at affection. Instead he broke off the kiss, hefted the bigger of the two packs and picked up his cloak. "Let's go."

Gailin hesitated, wanting to say goodbye to her grandmother. She feared in the pit of her stomach she would never again see the woman who had raised her and the thought brought tears to her eyes. She dare not let Drake see them and obedient to her mental command, they only burned and did not run down her cheek. A healer often must set aside her own emotions to help others with theirs. Instead, Gailin reached down and lugged her own pack after Drake, not even looking back, as if compelled.

"Where are we headed?" she managed to ask and then regretted ever making it his option. Before he could answer, she made her own wishes known. "Not into the mountains. They're so cold and I won't be able to grow anything there."

Drake looked back at her as he stood on the stoop considering their different options. He wouldn't want to go into the mountains either, she was reasonably sure. Drake knew that Vamilion was behind this abrupt play on the chess board they had been at for more than two decades. It left two directions open; northwest onto the plains or southeast, into the forest. Without asking further, Gailin brushed past him and began marching toward the sun, walking away from the river and out onto the grasses. Thankfully Drake didn't object. Perhaps he didn't care; just as long as they left before he had to confront the mountain man, whom he presumed was behind the power that had passed through the village and the haunting reappearance of a dead farmer.

Invisible and just beyond the verge of the forest, Vamilion watched them go. He tried desperately to tell himself that Gailin would be safer moving off. She was clever. Look how she had encouraged Drake to head out in the direction they planned to drive him. Her magic remained hidden and without hesitation she had left her grandmother and played the part demanded of her. She would be fine.

Wise Ones could only lie to themselves.

With a sigh Vamilion turned to the duty he had just inherited. The grandmother was now his to tend and he had little time to consider what he would do with this. He knew where his yearnings pulled him, but as was often the case, he doubted the purity of his own motives in taking Grandma to his home. But Vamilion wanted to go home and perhaps that was selfish. Paget would help there, certainly. It would give her something to do and it would be safer for the grandmother. He must remember to ask Gailin the next time he could, what was the poor old lady's name. Meanwhile he contemplated his options. He wanted to send the grandmother to his palace where Paget could wait on her. There she could be comfortable and cared for while Vamilion would be able to move more freely and would not be hindered and pinned down. Yes, he would send her there.

Resolved, he went into Gailin's cabin and found the pages the Queen had left for him, along with the old woman who was now his solemn responsibility. As he read the pages he surveyed the simple world Gailin had gleaned for herself. With a little inspection he found the herbs and supplements the healer had preserved and began to assemble them on the table in preparations to leave with them. He conjured a bag and then went to the chest for clothing for the old woman. He was almost done with his inspection when he heard a quavering voice from the bed nearest the fire.

"Gailin?" the old woman called weakly.

Vamilion knelt at the side of the bed and reached for the withered hand. "No, mistress. She is not here now. She has asked me to watch over you. You may call me Vamilion."

The old woman finally managed to open her eyes and focus on him. For his part, Vamilion felt the stab of the lady's green eyes and realized his mistakes in ever volunteering here. These were Gailin's eyes in sixty or seventy years. Despite the silvered hair, this would be Gailin's if she had never touched the Heart Stone and she would have aged just as beautifully as this frail woman. It wasn't a compulsion, but Vamilion acknowledged that the magic would drive him. He wanted so badly to go out onto the plains and see that woman just having looked at the soft and frail face of her grandmother.

Then the lady's hand gripped his fiercely, as if all her life resided in her gnarled hands. "No, your name is not that," she declared. "Why are you here?"

Vamilion could ask himself the same question. Why am I here? To watch over yet another woman dying, powerless and at the whims of time? Or was this practice for future deaths? Was every woman he ever knew doomed to die as he looked on? Strangely, he realized and for the first time in his life he was glad that both his children were boys. He thought of them; fine young men now with children of their own settling on the Lara River. They had left home as soon as they could under the uncomfortable realization that their father was an ageless magician and would never be able to live as other men. They would not forgive him for taking on the magic.

In a way Vamilion wouldn't forgive himself either, though he probably would make the same decision again, given the same dire circumstances. Twenty-five years earlier, he and his little family had been traveling along the coastline, kept out of the Land by the Seal. Then, for no discernible reason, the Seal had fallen. Their curiosity led the family to investigate and they began up the beach when magical explosions had frightened him and his family into hiding behind the doubtful shelter of their wagon. Owailion had come bolting across the beach to rescue them, offering him magic even as the explosions shattered their belongings. At the time, Vamilion would have done anything to avoid dying. Now he held the consequence. Responsibility for all the Land.

"Why am I here? I'm here to tend to you, mistress. I am going to take you to my home and watch over everything you need. Your granddaughter asked me to do this for her."

Something in his words must have contented the old woman, for her grip eased on his hand and she closed her eyes. "You're a good man," she declared before she abruptly fell back asleep.

With a sigh Vamilion rose back to his feet and then resolved, he stretched out his magical mind. He leaned toward the west, toward his home on the north side of the Vamilion Mountains. He felt the steady stones of the lower ridges and the tension there waiting for him to stir them awake. His presence brushed over the miners working in the deep roots, just discovering iron and tin in the veins there. Then he reached the tallest ridges and used its height as a lodestone for his magic. Then he slid his power down the slope, drawn in by something other than stone, but flesh and blood. Traveling this way was always easier when he reached for a mind. He reached for Paget.

He found her in the gardens of the grand palace called Vamilion, digging in the kitchen garden for something for her cooking. She had always been interested in the living things, not the cold and hard stones to which he felt akin. They had little in common now. She had followed him to the Land because at the time she had been a mother with two boisterous boys to raise and a husband who was away too often. He had been a trader, traveling the coastal routes between Demion and Marewn, and Paget had willingly packed up to follow him. But when the Seal on the Land had broken and new country demanded he defend it, Paget had little choice as her husband left her to become a Wise One. Now she was leaving him behind instead and nothing either could do would stop that change.

Vamilion couldn't consider the past when his present and future demanded his attention. He hated traveling like this but it couldn't be helped. With one portion of his mind he hefted the bed, occupant, conjured bag and all, and with the other he latched onto his wife's mind, with the mountain's peak as his fulcrum and he threw himself and the burden around through space. He and the bed landed right beside Paget, squashing the bean plants as she straightened up painfully from her harvesting. Vamilion immediately felt sick and curled over, vomiting into the garden row, trembling and holding onto the bedstead to keep from passing out.

At least Paget had grown accustomed to his strange arrivals. She dusted off her hands and reached for him, forcing him to sit and rest while the world spun around him, leaving him incapacitated for quite a while. She knew better than to demand an explanation for the bed and old lady that now occupied her summer garden. When Vamilion stopped retching, Paget wordlessly left and went inside the glossy wood door in the side of the grand palace and in moments returned with Goren, Vamilion's doorkeeper.

Goren, a steady, almost silent man also knew magic often deposited strange circumstances so he didn't question a bed in the garden. Instead he brought water for Vamilion while Paget pulled the lighter of the blankets up over the bolsters to shade the old woman from the sun until Vamilion was well enough to manage to get the bed inside the building that loomed over them.

Recovering must have taken quite a while, for the sun was lowering into his eyes by the time Vamilion's head stopped spinning and he managed to clamber up to sit on the foot of the bed. Paget and Goren stood in the beans waiting for an explanation and he had little to give them.

"I'm responsible for her until she dies," he managed. "I don't even know her name. I'll put her in the room on the ground floor."

Helpfully they stood him up and then he looked at the bed. Grandma seemed undisturbed by her thousand mile journey. He lowered the thin blanket to be sure she was still asleep. Then, with a practiced flick of his hand, she disappeared into the great palace, into one of its dozens of empty rooms. "Sorry about the beans," he commented, looking at the squashed vegetables and then over at Paget and Goren, who stood there watching him, mystified. "She is the grandmother of someone I found who is helping me deal with the hunter. I am supposed to guard Grandma until it is done or she dies naturally. This is how I was told to care for her."

He held the pages out to Goren who took them and began perusing them. Meanwhile Vamilion held out his arms toward Paget and she came to him, let him wrap his arms around her and give her a kiss, though her stiff smile warned him that he had more explaining to do. She knew he would not stay long and that she would want to talk before magic demanded that he leave her again.

Once inside his palace, Vamilion ate a hearty meal to recover his strength and then went to be sure Grandmother was comfortable. He spoon fed her the strange concoction Goren had prepared per Gailin's instructions. Then, after the old woman had fallen asleep again, he couldn't put it off any longer. He had to talk to Paget and explain what was happening in his life. He dreaded this conversation, knowing for twenty-five years after a fashion, it would come. He found his wife down in his work room dusting. She always cleaned when she was upset or stressed, and while his workshop always needed it, she would dust just to keep herself busy at this point.

"You've been cleaning," he commented dryly as he stood in the doorway, studying her single-minded work as her once white rag grew grey with the stone dust that coated every surface of his carving room. His present piece, a still shapeless lump of gray and blue veined marble, loomed in the corner, unacknowledged. "I'm sorry I couldn't come home sooner. Sometimes the compulsion is too hard to resist."

"I understand that," she replied without looking up from the sixth candle stick she had dusted. "You had to go."

Wordlessly he reached for her to still her determined dusting and held her hands in his until she stopped manically cleaning, though she still wouldn't look at him. In her mind he could hear how she didn't want to see his young face, sunburned and rugged. For his own part he noted how the tendons and veins in her hands showed more prominently than he remembered from just a month earlier. As a sculptor, he had been fascinated with hands and their qualities, but seeing hers changed so dramatically disturbed him. He also noted how the silver in her dark hair had grown more pronounced. He had probably given her every one of those grays with worry for him and he felt them like a stab in the heart.

"Paget, I need to tell you. Will you please sit?"

She turned toward him finally and glared, her snapping brown eyes again reminding him of the respect and love he had for this woman who had stayed with him throughout the tiresome demands of magic. She was perturbed, but it was nothing against him and she threw her rag down on the nearby table and sat down on a stool, unwillingly allowing him to explain what she probably already suspected.

"You knew it was a strong compulsion. I....I....I had to rescue her. But I didn't look at her. The compulsion was only to rescue. The spell to love her hasn't set in yet. I haven't even looked at her or heard her voice. The hunter followed me to her and is controlling her so she's in great danger. I'm communicating with her through writing so I won't be so... driven to be with her."

"Oh Gil," Paget interrupted him with a tone mixed with resignation and disgust, using the nickname she had used ever since they had met thirty-five years earlier in their native land. "You cannot go on this way. You've found her. She's in danger. Why are you doing this to yourself? To me? To her? You've got to go to her and the compulsion be damned."

"I made an oath to you," he reminded her. "I won't break that promise and..." He paused for he grew distracted as his clothing shifted into those of the King, regal and an annoying reminder of the magic that now dictated his life. Paget had seen it before and felt no alarm at the abrupt change.

"And you're a king, obviously. The kings of Demion have many wives," Paget pointed out, recalling for him their former life and homeland. "You're a King so magic is insisting that you can have more than one wife. She is meant to be yours. It's inevitable. Let me stay here contentedly and you go follow her to do magical things. It won't be a conflict any more. The boys aren't here to resent you and I...."

"Don't say it," he stopped her. "I need you and you need me."

Paget rolled her eyes to hide her pain. "You've given me everything I need. I'm old enough now the only thing I want is a warm bed and my comforts. Cleaning up after a dusty mountain man is more than enough work to keep me busy. You don't need to be here to shovel the snow any more. I've got Goren to do that. I'll take care of the grandma. You go do your magic work and let me do mine here."

Vamilion sighed. He hated the bitterness in her tone that belied her frank acceptance that really she had little comfort from his presence. "I don't want two wives, Paget," he replied gently. "Just because Demonia's kings feel this is fine, it's not right in my mind."

"Even when I cannot give you what a wife is supposed to give her young, vital husband?" she answered back. "That's not right either."

She wouldn't be so angry, he realized, if she were not trying to drive him away for his own sake. All the arguments they had endured in their marriage these last few years had primarily been over this issue, and he only now recognized that she was trying to push him away so he would not have to see her growing withered and less than desirable in his eyes.

Well, it wouldn't work, he acknowledged. Paget's attraction to him had little to do with her earlier luminous eyes and ebony hair, but more her bold mind, comforting presence and sharp wit. Those wouldn't fade for a long while, if ever, and he cherished them. She was like one of the jewels he often found in the deep roots of the mountains; hard and brilliant. Perhaps she had been more sparkly and polished earlier in their married life, but that didn't mean, with the clouding of her appearance, that she wasn't still a diamond in his hands. He remembered the facets and the purity.

"I do not need you for that, my love. I need you to be…my comfort, my reminder that I am human. With the evil I face… I need to know there is good in the world still." Then, despite her resistance, he pulled her into an embrace and held her there, as he slowly danced to music only he could still hear.

Chapter 9

Well Magic

Gailin's body ached and with her newly minted understanding of the human body, she did not doubt that the tendons in her feet would be enflamed by the time they walked the sun into the ground. She looked over the empty grasslands with a bleak eye. This was not her favorite place, she decided. It felt too exposed, especially with only Drake as a companion. He could murder her here in the grass and no one would ever find her body. She would molder and sink into the ground or be ripped to shreds by wild animals and no trace would be found.

Rather than dwell on these morbid thoughts, she decided it was time to try and engage her companion in a conversation. "Is it safe to talk now?" she began tentatively. "The villagers never come out this far onto the plains. We won't be seen...." She shouldn't have said that but now it was too late. Chiding herself for pointing out the obvious to him, she quickly continued. "I mean, we can talk about magic now, can we? You said you have a gift and so do I. What did you mean?"

Drake hadn't said a word as they had walked for the past three hours but her questions must have reminded him that she was with him, for he seemed startled. "The ropes. You broke them with magic. I saw that."

"That was the first time I had ever done magic," she said honestly. "I didn't think it would work, and it worked too well."

"It was impressive," Drake commented blandly. "But that was not why they thought you were a witch even before you escaped. Why were they hanging you?"

Gailin couldn't lie, even if she wanted to, so she admitted it. "I have a gift for healing that the villagers assumed was magical, so they accused me of being a witch when I couldn't save someone. I suppose the healing is magic, but I have had it all my life and was never trained....until now. Thank you for helping me learn." And she meant it, after a fashion. His hideous lessons in anatomy had helped her, and she knew Vamilion would never willingly teach her this way; face to face with open questions. Now she just had to use that knowledge of her magic against Drake. It would soon come time to start exploring the hunter's mind. She just had to draw him a little farther away from his link to the ley lines. Another day or two of walking?

"So, what kind of magical gifts do you have?" she asked innocently enough, hoping that her sharing would be enough to get him talking at last.

Drake looked at the setting sun and then stopped walking. "I have enough to know that this is as good as any a place to stop. If we're going to come out here, we'd better set up a camp of some kind. Then I can show you."

They cleared the dry grasses and Gailin twisted the gathered stems into sticks to burn in a fire, though she doubted they would last long enough to cook much. Drake used the knife he had put in his gear to dig a trough around a fire bed, but with only straw and grass as fuel, it seemed futile to Gailin. She watched him work at cutting his fire circle from the surrounding earth presumably to keep it from spreading into a grass fire. Then he stood back and rubbed his hands together. "This works better farther south," he commented and then placed his hand, palm down, firmly in the dirt he had cleared bare. He closed his eyes, concentrated and then began chanting an arcane spell. Gailin couldn't comprehend the language, for which she was grateful. The muttered words sent a shiver down her spine and she was grateful Vamilion had never required her to recite any mystical spells to do her magic.

Abruptly the dirt they had cleared erupted in flames. Drake pulled his hand back before he was burned, but Gailin rocked back with surprise. "That's amazing," she whispered, fascinated. His fire burned without fuel and when she tossed her manufactured sticks on the flames, the fire gobbled them up with little trouble and continued burning merrily along without growing any stronger.

"You'll be able to cook anything on that," Drake announced proudly. "The hard part out here will be getting water. We should have stayed close to the river. We might have to hunt as well, and there will be nothing out here so far away from the rivers."

"I can do water," Gailin supplied before she had even thought it through. She opened up her blanket-bag and pulled out the pot she had been cooking in since her childhood. It had come from Malornia with her grandmother and bore the fine quality that smiths here in the Land could not manage yet in their limited resources. Now she would use it as a magical reservoir. She set it on the fire and conjured water into it. "Soup for supper?" she asked with a smile, hoping the charm she doled out would distract him from curiosity about where her magic originated.

"Impressive," he commented with a strange look to his eye. "Have you done something other than water?"

Gailin knew she dare not reveal much. "I made the stylus I use to write in my book, but little else. Like I said, my gift has mostly been in healing; keeping my grandmother alive, gardening and breaking those ropes. Most of the training was in the medical areas and I've never met another magician before." All these things were meant to mislead him even though technically, they weren't lies. She had not 'met' Vamilion, and while he had trained her only a little, her instincts and own experimentation provided the bulk of her magical efforts. "I would love to learn more," she added, hoping to drive the conversation toward his revealing more about himself.

Drake sat beside his fire, concentrating on it, or fascinated by the flickering of the light as Gailin began adding ingredients from the food that they had brought from her house. She carefully let him see everything she did, easing any suspicion of her conjuring more than water. Best stay with elemental things like fire, water, wind and earth so that he would not realize she could have brought far more complex things into being. Was he feeling weakened already by the distance from the ley line that ran along the river? Should she make it seem that she too had to strain to tap into magic?

"Just keep him talking about his sorcery," rumbled a voice through her head. Owailion again? If so, she could relax this evening. He would warn her of anywhere she might misstep.

"What is there to learn besides herbs to heal, ropes to break or water to wash?" she asked frankly, hoping to break Drake's fire hypnosis.

"Can you listen into others' thoughts?" Drake commented.

Gailin's private mind smiled. "Is that possible?" Although she knew it for a true skill, she also needed the practice and working against Drake practically made her hungry to try.

Drake nodded, unaware of how she had not answered the question, but skillfully she avoided saying that yes, she could. Instead he replied, "And you'll need to learn to block thoughts as well. The two go hand in hand."

"Can you teach me?" she asked breathlessly.

Drake looked longingly at the soup as it bubbled away, full of the wonderful smells she could create with a few of her spices though the thin gruel only boasted a bit of onion and a potato. He seemed mesmerized by her hands stirring the soup and she realized he must be truly tired. Ley lines already? Her heart quickened at the thought. "Let's eat," she commented almost enticingly. "Then you can teach me."

"Good girl," Owailion rumbled through her mind.

Drake didn't reply but gladly took the bowl she served him and began eating greedily. Gailin had a difficult time keeping her speculative delight to herself. So he was already feeling the strain and needed to eat this way to keep up his energy. Sucking the life force off her wasn't enough if he were drawn far from the source of his magic. Despite the meal Drake still seemed lethargic and went to sleep almost as soon as the sun sank beyond the perfectly flat horizon.

Gailin, for her part remained awake and thanks to the full moon was able to write a few of her thoughts in the book. The plan is working, she wrote. Drake was obviously weakened and dependent on her. Then she asked how Vamilion was faring with her grandmother and finally she too went to sleep, although her mind was far too excited to settle until the stars had wheeled around and the almost wind finally stilled.

Deep in the night the moon had set and despite full summer, she felt a chill before she realized, with horror, Drake was touching her. His cold hand had wrapped around her throat. He wasn't squeezing, but the weight of his arm across her chest and the clammy grip made her shudder. She managed not to react or even gasp, but wondered how long he had been there draped across her. Slowly she turned her head to look at him and found him sprawled next to her, still asleep, completely unaware of the contact he had initiated. Was he more vulnerable this way? It didn't seem like he was even conscious. Perhaps his mind was open and unshielded now.

Greatly daring, Gailin reached toward Drake's mind as lightly as she could. Unlike Vamilion's thoughts which seemed strong and stable, Drake's felt like a labyrinth. She remembered the dream of wandering with Grandma through an oozing cesspool of evil, but this was different. He had the wall, like Vamilion, but it was a wall within a maze, crumbling and covered in moss and moisture. Even as she explored, the walls sank to the point she could see easily over them and she became aware of Drake's thoughts and dreams.

"She feeds me, feeds me. I don't have to kill her to feed. The others are not needed. The voices can stop. How can I keep her with me? If I feed on her, will they come and take her from me? No, I will not harm her. I will absorb her forever. She will be safe. She is mine. She feeds me. I'm so hungry."

The others? Gailin recalled all the souls she had found at the base of his mind and realized that the dream had shown her a truth. While that dream had been completely without tapping into Drake's thoughts, it had given her the path to go in and rescue the souls he had trapped inside himself. She realized he felt tormented by the voices of all the souls he had absorbed. Could she release them while he remained in this state? Something drove her to consider it. Was this the Wise One compulsion to help, urging her to take the risk of dipping deeper into the maze of Drake's mind? If so, she could only hope this worked.

And with Owailion's subtle, wordless encouragement, she decided to act. Taking a shallow breath, lest she wake him or move his hand off her neck, Gailin dove into the labyrinth. The walls still moldered and sagged. Sometimes she came across whole fallen walls and had to clamber over them. The path she had taken with Grandma corresponded almost exactly with the one she traveled now, though the environment wasn't so organic and literal like during the dream. She preferred moss and rock walls to veins and brain matter. And the light from the stars overhead remained her guide in this experience, but she could still feel Drake's cold hand, unflinchingly latched onto her neck. Chilled, she tried not to think of that.

Finally she came to the part of the path where the well of souls awaited her in the brain dream. However, here it appeared as a crumbling arch but the room beyond the walls seemed like a black void. No light passed in and while she could see over the walls on either side of the gateway, the void could not be observed unless she looked directly through the arch. She dare not enter in; why be foolish, ignoring her instincts. She had come to this dangerous place in his mind to release the souls. Again she sensed Owailion's encouragement and knew she needed to act. Would Drake be aware of her manipulation, awaken and attack her? She didn't feel like he would kill her, but he certainly would not appreciate her invasion.

Well, she had to do something. Carefully she conjured a metaphorical knife and reached toward the void, thinking of the darkness as a membrane similar to the one she had witnessed in the dream, stretched taut by the souls within straining to be free. She didn't want to touch it, but used the tip of the blade to reach out until she made contact with the darkness within the arch. Alarmingly the black film tore away with the least touch and a gray mist escaped, drifting away into the night sky.

The hand on her throat tightened, and Gailin withdrew her mind hurriedly.

"What did you do?" Drake gasped, his hand still on her throat, but he lifted his head, glaring at her with dark eyes. "You..."

She had a ready answer; hopefully one she would not get killed giving. "I was curious why you were touching me." It was an honest question. That she already knew and now understood more, that he was absorbing his life force from her didn't need to be said.

Drake rolled away from her, taking his offending hand with him and looked up into the sky. For the longest time he didn't say anything, just let the silence creep along the ground like a mist in a swamp. Gailin didn't interrupt his thoughts or tap in to hear what now she could sense from him with just a nudge. Instead she let him share what he was willing to reveal.

"I need you," he admitted. "I'm too far away from the ley lines."

"Ley lines?" she asked, implying she didn't know what he was talking about and perpetuating the falsehood that she was untrained.

"Where magic flows. It's strange, but you don't seem to be affected. I wonder why that is. Magic flows almost like rivers. And just like I need water, I need to be nearer it or I will get weakened magically. You, you're like a well, bringing the magic to the surface and I can walk here, far from the ley lines as long as you are near. I don't know why this works but it does."

"Where are these ley lines? Can you see them?"

"No, they aren't visible, but sorcerers can sense them. It's one of the major things I am doing here in the Land: mapping the lines for others to come. Other magicians will want to know and then I can sell that information to them in trade for something I need." His eyes flicked to his cloak where presumably he had the map he had built. He wasn't ready to share it with her though he was easily teaching her about ley lines nonetheless. And the walls of his mind had strengthened accordingly. This was a secret he wanted to keep close; valuable to him like buried jewels.

"What would happen if the lines went away?" she asked curiously, hiding her fear of what that map would do to the Land.

"It's impossible. They are like rivers. The magic must flow. You would have to break the ground open and have magic fall back to the center of the earth to make the ley lines fade."

"So why can you still do magic even out here, far away from ley lines that I cannot even sense?" she asked innocently.

Drake sighed wistfully. "I don't know. I simply tap into you and... Your magic is different. You block naturally. You can draw water up and you can heal, both of which are great examples of magical power, but rare. Can you read minds?"

"I think that's what I was doing, trying to find out why you were touching me. You were thinking you were hungry."

Drake looked over at her and smiled for the first time since they had met. "Hungry? I suppose I am hungry; magically hungry that is. I usually tap into the ley lines through the people who live near them, but with you, I can go other places, even far from people. If the lines are rivers, you are drawing from a well, tapping into the magic that is deeper than the river. Maybe you broke your ropes at the hanging with such spectacular results because you didn't use the ley lines at all, but the well magic."

"Well magic?" she speculated. "Is it more powerful than ley lines, or just different?"

Drake looked back at the stars with curiosity. "Again, I don't know, I've never met a magician who used it, but it's an interesting concept. I'd like to see how it works because until now I've never been able to tap into someone else's magic this way. I seem to be able to use magic with you as the conduit. We should look into it. I need you....out here I would die without being able to use the ley lines."

"Die? Aren't you able to live without magic? You are human, right? I went almost all my life without magic and no one ever questioned what I needed to live."

"Ah, but you were born and lived near the ley lines. You tapped into them without even thinking about it," he qualified. "You don't know what it's like to live away from them."

"I'm living away from them now and I don't feel any different," she commented and then privately chided herself for ever revealing this.

"You will," he promised. "You will indeed feel different. Now, do you have anything for a headache? I've got a terrible throbbing in my head and it's almost dawn."

Chapter 10

Pressure

Vamilion spent a week at home, settling Grandma and apologizing to Paget, but he felt guilty for ignoring his magical duties the entire time. The compulsion to protect his future wife as well as do his half of the plan was at work and he had a niggling sense that the Land was in eminent danger. Owailion had the watch over Gailin, so that left Vamilion with the protection of the Land, or at least the most likely approaches. With magicians on the way, he could not remain at peace, even at home. And home was hardly peaceful. While she never said anything, Paget's cleaning and hovering over Grandma nagged him wordlessly. Paget wouldn't speak of her disquiet but she had told him she didn't need him with her actions. He was left in his work room chiseling away at a lump of stone and felt useless.

Finally, when he couldn't stand the pressure any longer, he announced that he was leaving and Paget saw him off at dawn of the final day with a hug, but no kiss and she walked back into the palace without a word. Vamilion couldn't understand his emotions at this cold, frank departure. So, without answers, he latched onto the far western peak at the edge of the Vamilion Mountains and shifted away, as unsettled as a volcano.

Traveling mountain to mountain was effortless and had no ill side-effects for him and Vamilion was able to move instantly three hundred miles to the edge of the chain without pain. Then he simply sat on the ridge to think. Behind him dawn had not reached this far west and he watched the summer sky lighten as he looked below at the Laranian River winding to the sea beyond him. The green snaking water reminded Vamilion of Drake for some reason and he distrusted its placid nature. Something lurked below and he could not begin to comprehend it now, not with being so unsettled.

That brought to mind the tale of Raimi, Owailion's Queen of Rivers. Vamilion never met her, but it would have been her responsibility to keep sorcerers from coming to the Land via the rivers and now her skills were lost, leaving the Mountain King and Owailion, the King of Creating, to do her work. If he squinted into the glare off the water Vamilion could see Raimi's palace, built after her death, on an island in the delta of the river. It gleamed like a diamond, the hope Owailion retained for her resurrection, but remained empty and cold even in the summer light. The legends said that when all sixteen of the Wise

Ones had taken their place in their palace, becoming Seated, that the Land would again be sealed and no magic would dare again attack. The problem was Raimi was dead. Would there ever be someone to replace her? Not in Owailion's heart. He was bitter and practically a hermit in his grief over her. And while Owailion would come to the aid of the Land at need, he did not do it willingly.

That thought led Vamilion to consider what his fellow Wise One would do to guard this river. They had agreed to split the duties: Vamilion on the Laranian and Owailion on the Don. It seemed unfair that, here he was, stuck on a mountaintop watching a river because this was as close as he could get magically. There must be something better he could do to stop outlander sorcerers from invading. But what?

Vamilion turned toward the southwest, hoping to see a ship that oozed evil magic. No such luck. He saw only a few fishing boats and trade vessels bringing timber down river to build up the docks and villages along the southern part of the delta. The lower half of the Laranian had been slow to develop. It was swampy now, since Raimi's death, and most of the immigrants had elected to go farther up the river to where the mountains brought down fresh water, nurturing forests and better farmland. With so few people here at the delta, it was vulnerable to invasion. How could Vamilion prevent a magical influx when mountains would only interfere with the flow of the water? He would do more harm than good for the people of the Land by blocking the flow or lifting and draining the marsh.

What he needed was some way to block the mouth of the river from all unwanted traffic. How? Owailion had forbidden him changing the actual geography of the Land even if it was well within his capability. The elder magician had muttered something about hidden magic in very specific places and if Vamilion fiddled with the bedrock some of the secrets would be lost. In other words, don't change the mountains. Vamilion's inner rebel grated against the restriction. It would be wonderful to have a lone peak in the middle of the plains to make travel easier, but that would be interference to some other Wise One's Seeking sometime in the future.

Vamilion looked out to sea now and could not make out where the ocean and sky met. They were the same color and bright in his eyes. He might not be able to make changes on the land, but what about the sea? It was from the sea where the invaders approached. Every danger on land, he could block because of his connection to the stone beneath, but danger still most often came by sea. Someday there might be a King or Queen of the Sea, but until then, Vamilion had a duty to guard the waterways from invasion.

Without meaning to, he pressed his mind down into the roots of the mountains and sensed the fault lines that had crafted the Vamilion Mountains after which he was named. They plunged under the river and then turned abruptly out to sea. The heavy weight of the gulf water did little to inhibit his probing mind and he felt the tension in the two plates pressed against each other. They might slip against each other, but what would happen if he forced the direction down on the smaller plate? He could bring up a volcano. The heat of a melting plate would rise and he could craft a mountain at the mouth of the river to guard the way. The faults were set already for such a move and it would not interfere with any of Owailion's secrets hidden somewhere in the Land. It would only form an island to guard the way just beyond the mouth of the Laranian River.

Almost with a compulsion, Vamilion began the pressure needed to force one plate under the other. An earthquake under the water created a wave, but he suppressed it before it could wash ashore and the boats never noticed a change other than they had some extra tacks to make as they came into the mouth of the river. The heat rose and Vamilion's magic burned and cracked like iron in a forge. He felt the magma rising and bubbling onto the surface of the ocean bottom. It would take weeks to get the volcano to break the surface, but he had nothing but time, sitting on his mountain, watching for invaders and hoping to block them with a guarding island.

With that working, he reluctantly pulled out the tablet that he had been using to communicate with Gailin. He hadn't looked in three days and felt a little guilty for avoiding her questions. He trusted Owailion to keep her safe, and while he wanted to resist growing closer to her, he also wanted to learn how it went dealing with the snake. He wanted to reject his curiosity. He could justify ignoring her, but he didn't want to. He needed to keep up with her world even as he alienated her. With a wave of his hand the tablet revealed all she had written in the past week since she left for the plains with Drake.

And what he read sent a shiver down his spine .

She was learning amazing things about the ley lines and the magicians that tapped into them. She now knew more about Wise One magic than Owailion or Vamilion had suspected. Well Magic was a new concept to him. And now she was plotting how to get the map of the ley lines from Drake or at least share it with Vamilion. She even implied that breaking the ley lines might be possible. Also she had successfully released some of the souls from within the hunter. However, in order to gain this close connection, nurturing his trust and knowledge, she had to allow Drake to touch her and had been bonding with him in ways that made Vamilion physically ill.

With his magical eye, Vamilion tapped into the past and saw for himself how Drake's hand had gravitated toward her throat. The King of Mountains wandered like a ghost through the sorcerer's mind maze, observing the corrosive and yet crumbling walls. He watched Gailin's hand slice free the souls within the snake. This patient work she performed would eventually make victory possible but Vamilion struggled with his own impatience and felt like throttling Drake for allowing his hand to linger evocatively on the neck of the girl he would one day call his wife. If she felt fear of the monster, or worse, attraction, it made Vamilion's gorge rise. He found himself wanting to abandon his post and challenge the snake. Maybe it was a good thing that Vamilion didn't have the gift of instant travel or he would have done just that.

And Owailion was allowing, even encouraging this? Of course he was. Owailion would have seen nothing wrong with permitting or at least justifying Gailin's attraction for Drake. He wanted them together so that she could learn all there was to know about their potential invaders. Keeping Drake off center, weakened and vulnerable, was only part of it. Probably the oldest Wise One also wanted to show Vamilion all he was risking by not bonding solely to Gailin and thus exposing her to this danger. It would be poignant justice if she were compromised or killed because of Vamilion's abandonment.

Vamilion's ire made the volcano he was crafting lurch explosively and he had to hurriedly squelch another tsunami before it got out of hand. Then he turned back to look at Gailin's thoughts behind the words. She didn't express much emotion in her writing; a healer to the core, he realized. She would not let her revulsion or attraction interfere with the task at hand. However, Vamilion couldn't help but read between the lines, wondering if she wanted Drake to touch her. Was she lonely or attracted to the idea of a man wanting her to the point that she would allow his flirtations and courting to flatter her? Many a woman wanted a man, any man, just for the sake of having one. Especially since Vamilion had rejected her, would she gravitate to Drake?

Again Vamilion felt his frustration get ahead of his wisdom. He didn't feel anger toward Gailin. That seemed impossible given the compulsion he felt toward her. She was the victim. But he felt something and it had no outlet but that volcano. He had to direct his discontent toward something more worthy of being fought. He couldn't take it out on Drake who would simply kill Gailin the instant he sensed Vamilion's attack. The only other resource for venting his frustration was Owailion...who wasn't even watching over Gailin at the moment.

Vamilion stretched out his mind and found his fellow Wise One at the mouth of the Don River working with settlers there to build two fortresses, one on each shoreline to house soldiers against the invasion there, the third wave Owailion anticipated. Vamilion interrupted with a thought.

"You aren't protecting the Queen," he barked at his colleague mentally, distracting him from carefully setting a stone using non-magical means. "You are setting her up to be...to be..." Even in his mental tone, Vamilion was sputtering, unable to launch his anger with enough pressure to satisfy. Words didn't fall like an avalanche and Owailion was safely far from the nearest mountain.

"So you noticed," Owailion drawled, hardly fazed by the volume and ire directed at him. He kept his eye on the catapult crane the men were working to lift a stone as he simultaneously replied. "It was your choice. You won't look her in the eye and abandon yourself to loving her. So I'm protecting her from you as much as him. She is valuable to him now and he won't kill her because of it. That's protection enough."

Vamilion fumed. "And what is your plan to get her out? Are you keeping her from... from being taken advantage of? She won't kill him, at least not willingly. She will feel like she can disable him and render him harmless instead. She doesn't realize she will have to kill him eventually and she won't want to be the one to rip his brain apart since she's wandering so freely within it. She's going to fall in love with him."

Vamilion could feel Owailion's sincere doubt in the inaudible scoffing. "No, and I have every confidence that she will have no problem killing him," Owailion replied frankly. "She'll do it if you or I are in danger. She will commit herself to the cause of the Land or she will be lost to us. She will not ever be torn the way you or I have become. She will only have one path."

"You're a..." Vamilion couldn't think of a good enough word for Owailion's manipulation and cold, cruel pragmatism. For the first time, the language of the Land failed him and he ripped off a string of curses in Demonian for Owailion's benefit before he cut off the contact.

Somewhere two thousand miles away on another river Owailion smiled as the next stone was set in a tower. Plans were coming into place quite nicely.

Through the weeks they walked and Gailin used
well magic to provide for them the whole way. Sh
deliberately didn't conjure grand things and instead
gathered carefully from the land around them. She
harvested wild grain by hand for porridge in the
morning and magically provided the water for the
cooking as if this was the most she could provide. The
salt and honey they had brought with them when
they left on this journey didn't quite seem to run out
for some odd reason and she hoped Drake didn't notice. The rabbits and groundhogs they were able to
catch in snares they set at dusk always managed to
get trapped rather easily so there was always meat in
the pot at the end of the day. Drake didn't complain
or comment. He still didn't know the extent of her
magic and she wanted to keep it that way.

However, at night he slept with his arm across her,
pinning her and taking his energy from her like a
thirsty man from the only watering hole for a hundred miles. His seductive touch still chilled her, like
a reptile had climbed across her shoulders, twining
around her neck and subtly squeezing, not quite cutting off her breathing; a burning cold necklace of
threat. She dare not move in her sleep and she spent
her nights desperately hoping his hand did not slip.
One night she tried to roll over onto her side with
her back to him, but his hand slid onto her hip and
he pulled her close, almost snuggling, and she didn't
do that again. While he seemed devoid of emotion or

passion, she wouldn't put it past him to rape her just to absorb more energy from her fear and pain.

So she remained sleepless most of the trip, managing on only one or two hours at most. She used the dark hours to delve into his mind, mapping how it worked and making up for all the parts of the anatomy she had been unable to study in a live human. She knew his past, his memories, his senses, even his magic, like it was her own. She possessed everything but his name. If she wanted, she could render him blind or deaf with a little flash, burning one connection in his brain, leaving the rest intact. On a regular basis she traveled down to the well of souls and cut open the void again, releasing a few more, but this activity always resulted in headaches in the morning so she didn't push for all of them to escape at once. The barrier encasing them sealed itself up almost instantly so she doubted Drake would notice the loss.

Dare she strip him of his memories? Could she steal his name from him? Was it possible to make him forget that he knew her name? She felt capable of it, but not until she had freed the last soul within. Then she would call Vamilion and Owailion and attack, but only once she knew it was safe. You did not cut that chord until you were sure.

So in the meanwhile she plotted how to get the map from Drake. She nightly pulled it out of his cloak but he had made the writing invisible and she put it back as she found it, still thinking how to get its secrets without his knowing. He never looked at the parchment that she was aware of and she doubted he would notice if she replaced it with a fake but that didn't give her a way to read it. Finally she did replace it one night with an identical and absolutely blank roll of parchment. But what to do with the blank map? She dare not keep it with her and after one day of travel with it placed next to her invisible Heart Stone, she decided to send it to Vamilion. Sending the parchment might be an interesting exercise in magic she had not tried yet.

With concentration, and the sky perfectly dark, devoid of moon and stars obscured under a thin veil of cloud, she reached out, hoping to feel a brush of the solidity she found in Vamilion's mind. Her trek across the plains had brought her progressively closer to the Great Chain of mountains and she used them to feel for him.

"Vamilion?" she called, using hope as the spark to reach for him. It seemed the only thing she could manage with her throat closed off by Drake's hand. It took longer than she hoped and she began to fear that he was out of her range, or she was misdirecting her call. Surely the mountains knew where he was. Then, far and echoing, as if it bounced between the mountain ranges, she heard a reply.

"Gailin, is this safe?"

She could have wept for joy at the mind voice he provided to her. The comforting strength and solid patience of it brushed aside the clinging cool of the reptile touch on her mind. Vamilion's protective thoughts leapt out to her first. He was immediately worried for her. His mental majesty lifted her soul and she realized that yes, she did feel different for her constant contact with the sorcerer. She had forgotten how it felt to be warm, clean and strong. Even when she was alone and without magic she felt better than being used and absorbed by Drake. Vamilion's caring voice reminded her of that.

"Yes, I think. He....he..."

"I will crush his brain for you. The instant he touches you...the instant you think it is safe. Please say you are safe."

"Safe, no. I am not safe, but I am not in immediate danger. I have the map to the ley lines that he has created. He should not keep it. I've traced his mind and can eliminate the memory of it if need be, but I want you to take the map. It might be of use some day."

"What will happen when he realizes you have taken it?" Vamilion asked, seeking something conversational so he didn't find himself climbing down the peak to be with her.

"I'm hoping he doesn't realize it's missing. He never opens it because there are no ley lines here for him to mark. He is barely functioning and does no magic because he cannot really do more than survive off the energy I'm giving him. But we soon will reach the mountains, where there are ley lines for him to tap. That will be the true test. Will he need me anymore? I think he will keep me, but by then hopefully I will have released all his souls. He'll be hungry then and will have to kill again. That will be when we must be ready."

She could hear Vamilion's palpable sigh of resignation. He wanted to come to her rescue, a gallant knight in shining armor, but he knew that would not help. While it was charming, she knew it for a whimsical thought. "I'll see what I can do to make his ink visible. In the meantime… I'll throttle Owailion for you instead."

"Why? He's been very supportive." She almost gasped at the rancor she heard in Vamilion's mental voice.

"Because he got you into this mess. It was his suggestion. I would never have tolerated sending you off with a Soul Eater to cross the plains if I had known he would not follow you more closely. There has to be a better, safer way to strip Drake of your name. Owailion doesn't really worry about your protection. He only wants to learn from him all about the invasion and…"

"Invasion?" Gailin interrupted.

"Yes, your snake there, he is the scout for the two other magical invasions. That's my job; to counter the first wave when they arrive while Owailion prepares for the second. It shouldn't be long now. They must suspect Drake is in trouble and are coming because they haven't heard from him. He is probably planning on giving them the map so they know where they can safely invade and we must be ready. I might have to give him the map back to keep you safe, but I will change the lines and see how they fare out in the middle of the plains far away from their lifeblood."

"How can I help?" she asked, desperate for some way to be of service.

"Help? You are doing more than you know. You are mastering magic very quickly and keeping their spy in check. It's more than Owailion or I can do right now. We are waiting for the hammer to fall and preparing. You are already fighting. Do not fret for us. Your battles will come."

"Very well. Here is the map. I've replaced it with a simple blank piece of parchment. Tell me when you have a false map or at least can read what he has created."

And with that she threw the rolled up scroll with her mind, following the echoing magic of the King of Mountains.

"I've got it, my..." and he interrupted himself before he added the word that would make it an endearment. Instead he finished awkwardly, "I'll tell you when I've broken his spell. Sleep well."

Chapter 11

Lines Crossed

Vamilion looked at the roll in his lap but didn't really see it. Instead he wondered at the strength of the connection he felt for Gailin despite the distance he had maintained. He almost slipped there. And his desire to strangle Drake felt more powerful than it ever had when the snake had only threatened himself. Now that Gailin was the target, Vamilion found himself seeking for reasons to pound the sorcerer to dust. If he already felt so protective for a lady who really had probably more skill at defeating the snake than even he did, how far had he come? He cared for her more than he wanted to admit. And he was angry for her sake as well, at Owailion even. This was not a good position to be in if he were going to last for another twenty years or so until Paget died. How was he going to endure? Maybe if the stress of defending Gailin and the Land were to ease and he could go back to being a sculptor? Perhaps if Gailin were off doing typical Seeking things without being in constant danger of being commanded to die, he would feel less of a compulsion toward her.

Or maybe not. Maybe he was doomed no matter that he had never seen Gailin nor spoken with her in person. And maybe the world would stop spinning too. Anything was possible, but this compulsion was only going to grow stronger and twenty or more years were not going to be easy.

To distract himself, Vamilion unrolled the parchment and began to study what might be there. He tasted the magic with a mental touch, seeking the root of the spell on the page. Like the ley lines, he could sense something there despite his eyes seeing nothing. He brushed his roughened hands over the paper and recognized the outline of the Land under his seeking fingers, but the frequency of certain lines seemed different than he knew. As the most skilled cartographer especially in ley lines in the Land, he knew his own work when he felt it and Drake had utilized his original drawings somehow. Had copies of his original geologic surveys made it to other lands? If so, how? And how was he going to see what intentionally had been hidden.

Vamilion decided not to try to force the magical ink to appear but instead thought of his experiments with iron and lodestones. He knew iron filings reacted to the magnetic pull of a lodestone and would congregate in grooves where the density of any substance had grown thicker because of pressure, even the slight pressure of a pen. Could he get the iron dust to settle in the lines of this parchment and cling there?

With the distraction of a challenge, Vamilion began conjuring. First he created a deeper shelf in the mountainside so he could work more comfortably. He had been sleeping in a tent up here on the ridge, but this work required more precision than clinging to a mountainside would allow. Then he enlarged his tent and crafted a table and chair so he could work on a flat surface. For better light he conjured a miner's lantern and set to work. Lumps of shale held down the curling corners of the map. A bottle of the finest iron filings appeared in his hand and he poured a small portion into his palm. He had never actually done this and had to use magic to make the finest dusting fall evenly across the parchment. With a gentle breath he blew the filings into the air above the map and then let gravity take over.

When the dust settled and he felt he had an even coating, invisible to the naked eye, Vamilion conjured his lodestone. The slightly gray haze that had fallen onto the parchment began to shift and shimmer as he passed the loadstone under the table. Like true magic instead of physics, the filings danced and trembled, straining to get out of the lines into which they had fallen. They marched like soldiers, upright in all the lines that spider-webbed across the paper. And much to his surprise, there were more lines than he ever thought; at least double. He looked at the paper with wonder. Out of curiosity he reached out his mind and scooped up the map that remained in his study in the palace in the east so he could compare the two.

As his personal map arrived he had to admit his own map of ley lines was almost worthless in comparison. For every line he had drawn he saw two others that crossed in graceful arcs. These extra lines might be shorter but far more prolific. Obviously Vamilion had not followed every lead when he had drawn his ley line map. With the shorter lines he saw on Drake's map, Vamilion most likely had followed the stronger pull and ignored a shallower nudge. Indeed, most of the new lines intersected or crossed with his original larger ones. Well, he thought, this was worth exploring and he might do so if he didn't have responsibility for stopping an invasion and worry for a Queen to occupy his thoughts. Maybe he could investigate with those twenty plus years he had until Paget passed.

Vamilion felt disgusted for even thinking about Paget's death with anticipation. That was wrong and he knew it. Instead of chiding himself, however, he conjured himself a separate colored stylus to mark the additional lines onto his first map and then made another copy for Owailion who would also find it of interest. Now all he had to worry over was how to help Gailin with the map. Should they give the original map back to the snake and he would never know they had it? Or could they use the loss of the map to be the challenge against him, inciting the battle that would ensue and result in finally killing the despicable sorcerer?

Undecided, Vamilion sent an extra copy to Owailion. He would wait until night to speak again with Gailin to decide how he was going to deal with the new revelation about the ley lines, and the danger there. Most alarmingly, one of the newly discovered lines dipped deeply into the plains, and Gailin would come dangerously close soon.

Unfortunately, life had other plans for him.

* * *

In the middle of the night she felt a gentle nudge and at first Gailin thought Vamilion must be getting back to her about the map. But there were no words coming with the awakening. Drake's hand was in its customary place, and while he was practically draped all across her, he was also sound asleep so he could not be the source of the prompting. The sky above her remained pitch black, but the mist across the grasses spoke of dawn approaching and perhaps the first sign that fall would descend soon. The fog seemed to dance, calling to her to walk.

Greatly daring, Gailin wriggled out from under Drake's hand and set it gently on the imprint of where she'd been laying and stood up. Once on her feet the starlight lit the mist for her, showing her the way down a shallow gully north of their camp and she knew she must follow the path. It felt like one of those compulsions Vamilion had left with the book. However, she had left the book behind in the camp, knowing Drake would find nothing in it of worth to him; just drawings of herbs and anatomy. She could have resisted this prompting to follow the mist but now was a perfect time so she waded into the grasses, guided by a fog bank.

Once in the gully the mist had gathered so thickly that she could not see the night above her head and she might be on another planet for all she could make out in the murk. The prompting nudged her down the path of the dry wash that probably had been cut only by summer thunderstorms. No stones tripped her but a few sparse, desperate attempts at trees pushed out of the ground, hardly more than bushes and she had to weave her way through them before she reached where the mist prompted her to go.

Then she saw a light within the fog. It didn't seem to have any one source but appeared as if the mist itself began to glow just a bit farther down the path. She approached cautiously, suspicious of a trick, but the clarity of the light and ease of the compulsion reassured her. She wasn't being driven against her will. The glowing grew so intense she felt blinded and didn't dare step closer until she studied out the situation. She stopped and considered all she had learned about magic. The light and the prompting meant she should be here, but she found herself blocked until she understood what the magic demanded of her.

She thought of the veil over the well of souls in her dream, how it stretched and yet had resisted breaking until she pierced through the material, yet it had all been metaphorical. This veil of nothingness required her to break through with magic of her own. Perhaps this brightness was much the same and she needed to break through. Without hesitation Gailin conjured a scalpel and reached forward, cutting the light with a swift stroke. Where her weapon passed, a lavender gash in the mist appeared. Gailin followed her instinct and carefully reached her hand into the fissure she had caused. The mist burned her skin like alcohol in a cut but the smell of lavender permeated the early morning and she refused to flinch back from the pain.

Then her reaching hand felt something solid within the fog bank. A smooth cylinder, cool to the touch, but not metallic and she grasped it, pulling it free from the opening in the light. Much to her surprise she had withdrawn a thick white candle. It had no dripping marks to indicate it had ever been used and its size made it almost too cumbersome to grasp with one hand. The obviously magical hiding of it assured her that it was meant for her, but she had never seen anything less exceptional unless the sheer size of the candle was magical as well.

What had Vamilion said about certain Talismans hidden all over the Land? Could this be one of them? If so, what did it do? She was, after all, a Seeking Queen and had been given a mandate to master her magic, finding these Talismans and eventually become Seated in a grand palace somewhere here in the Land. Oddly enough this was the first indication she had that the Land still expected her to be something other than Drake's victim.

The thought of him waking without knowing where she was spurred Gailin to action. She couldn't put the candle in her pocket like the Heart Stone and expect it to go unnoticed, so without thinking, she wove an invisibility over it and then imagined up a bag at her back where she could hide things such as her book, the Heart Stone and now this candle so that no one would know it was there. She put the candle in the bag, slung it over her shoulder and then began tramping out of the mist the way she had come. By the time she reached the top of the swell, the mist had faded and dawn was coming, burning away any trace of where she had been.

Unfortunately Drake was awake when she returned. He sat in the trampled grass of their camp waiting for her with a strange gleam in his eye, half anger, and half curiosity. While it wasn't uncommon for her to leave, most often to use the privy or to gather grain for breakfast, he always knew when she had left. Before she reached his side, she conjured the expected gleanings into her pocket and came into camp as if nothing was out of the ordinary. She broke out the pot as if she were going to make their porridge and looked at him in surprise when he didn't start up the fire as was his custom.

"Where were you?" he demanded.

Rather than tell him the truth, she brought water into the pot and replied, "Where do you expect I was? The morning was beautiful with the mist. We might be coming into the fall. We need to reach a village before the weather turns."

Drake still did not respond as expected. "You left me," he accused.

"You were safe," she reminded him. "We are coming back to the mountains and there might be some ley lines there."

"Let me see," he replied coldly and Gailin abruptly realized her mistake. He held up the roll of parchment that he had been hiding behind his back. His anger bristled, showing her his sharpened teeth like his forked tongue. He had discovered her replacement map. Gailin felt the drip of fear down her throat but before she could react, he invoked name magic.

"Gailin, you will not call for help. Gailin, you will not use magic on me. Gailin, you will not move." His words came so quickly she could not react in time. Instead she froze where she stood, eyes wide in alarm.

"Why?" she gasped, as if she were ignorant of his motives. "I've done nothing but help you."

Drake rose from his seat and came toward her, slapping the useless parchment into his shaking palm. Slowly he circled around her and seductively drew the tip of the scroll around her neck like a knife. She managed to swallow. "You are a magician," he whispered. "You have powers. Why should I trust you?"

"I cannot lie to you," she replied, "but I have no way to prove it to you."

This surprised him and he stopped circling her. The offending parchment disappeared and he placed his hand against her throat and his face so close to hers that she would have backed up if she were able. He leaned in and kissed her violently, his hands groping all over her body and her mind screamed in hor-

145

ror. He was going to rape her right there. But then abruptly he stepped back.

"Gailin, look at yourself," he commanded.

Her head regained enough control that she was able to look down and saw something even more amazing than any of the magic she had witnessed up until that time. Running all down her body she wore a lavender silk gown embroidered with silver lilies. Over the diamond and silver embellishments she wore a steel baldric from which hung a crystal quiver and white fletched arrows. She looked down the flowing sleeves that almost brushed the ground and found she also held a silver bow in one hand and in the other, the candle she had just found.

"Now Gailin, tell me why I should trust you. You are a Wise One," Drake snapped even as he stood back to admire the effect of her mysterious change.

"Which means I cannot lie. It's impossible. I've tried," in despair she replied. Oh, please, Vamilion, now would be a wonderful time for you to call me and give back the map, she thought privately though she still could not send the thought out with any magic.

Drake began his pacing around her again, treading on the skirt that flowed out behind her like water. "It seems you are right, you cannot lie. You see, this is a truth spell I've put on you. Your appearance is as you truly are. I see lilies and diamonds but nothing to indicate where your power is focused. The mountain king is obvious when he changes... but not you. What is your power? Gailin, tell me."

With a sigh she replied. "I am the Queen of Healing. I basically told you that already. My gift is for understanding how the human body works and how to heal it."

"Hummm, not as impressive as mountains, I fear," Drake's voice drawled. His confidence and arrogance was back. Perhaps they had traveled close enough to a ley line that he could draw from that now. "No, the others are more intimidating. You are too delicate and frail. They must not think much of your power if they will allow you to come alone out here with one such as me."

Gailin felt none of the envy in her fellow Wise Ones like Drake implied. Indeed, she barely knew Vamilion and had only brief comments from Owailion so Drake's stab at her lack of powers did nothing to raise her jealousy. Perhaps as a Wise One she could not truly feel envy toward her peers. Instead the fear of her capture brought out a stubborn bold anger at her predicament.

"What do you look like in a truth spell?" she snapped back, letting anger come out rather than her fear. Accordingly he slipped his hand back around her throat and began squeezing.

"You don't want to know," he replied frankly in a hiss that reminded her of the tongue she had often seen flicking between his teeth when she wasn't thinking about it. "But it might reassure you to learn that I don't want to kill you. I could slaughter you with a word, you know."

"Yes, I know," she whispered with what little breath she could gather. She wanted to keep him engaged because speaking with him meant he wasn't doing other things to her and time was on her side. Vamilion would check in, or perhaps Owailion and they would hear the alarm in her mind and know she needed their help.

"Do you know what I want from you?" he asked, easing his hand slightly and drew her face toward his ever so slightly. As if her stoic glare released something in him, her appearance went back to her simple dress and apron. It made her feel more capable of fighting him despite the fact that she had not regained her ability to move. It put them back on their formerly equal level.

"Gailin, you will bear me a son."

The slamming weight of name magic came thundering down on her like an avalanche and she staggered despite the prohibition to moving. His hand on her neck kept her upright. She writhed in her head, hoping for a way to escape although such a long term directive seemed impossible to fulfill. Why would he want a son? He cared for nothing; not her, not the Land, not himself except for the magic he could wield. Gailin could only think of one motive he had.

"To pass on the magic?" she asked frankly, swallowing carefully against his sticky hand over her trachea, ready to cut off her air once again.

"Who better? The magic of the Wise Ones is the most formidable in all the world but until now it has come only to the Land and only to males. We thought maybe there would be no more female Wise Ones but now I have the evidence. My colleagues will allow my seed to be the experiment to see if we can breed the most powerful magicians the world has known. And you will be mine, won't you Gailin?" It wasn't a question, but a factual statement. He knew he had won.

"You know that even with name magic, I might not be able to bear a child. And any child might be a girl. It might not…" he squeezed her voice off and she stopped before she could point out the many things that made his goal beyond her control.

"I'm sure you, with your understanding of the body, can manage to be sure you conceive and it is a son. Now, shall we proceed?" and he placed his hands on her hips possessively.

Gailin looked longingly to the north, wishing the mountains were more than a grey line where the sky met the horizon. Then she remembered that towns and villages were there. Perhaps someone else could help her. She grasped at the hope.

"Do you want your son to be a bastard? I must marry you first."

Drake also looked over toward the north, surprised by the suggestion. It had been a long time since he had slept in a bed and fed on souls instead of Gailin's steady stream of well magic. His lust dwelt at many levels and none of them were met by groveling here in the grass. He nodded, removed his hands from her body and then began gathering up their belongings. When she didn't move to help him, he sighed and said the words. "Gailin, you can move again."

She dropped to her knees and with shaking hands began to pack. He would at least do this right. She used her reprieve to magically scribble a comment in the book about Drake but because of the prohibition set on her she could not set a compulsion to read it on the words. Instead she made a running list of her thoughts as they packed up and began walking toward the northern horizon as if nothing had changed. And yet everything had.

Over the day Gailin began to come to a somewhat peaceful conclusion that this was probably the best she could hope for. If she didn't think about his magic and just Drake as a man, she wasn't displeased. Of course she wanted to love, or to at least care about the man she married. She might have thought much the same of Jonis. Drake wasn't repulsive physically and while she didn't love him and disliked his cold personality, he wouldn't beat her or abuse her, drink or womanize like other men might. More than once her grandmother had told her that in a place like the Land, so recently settled, a girl didn't have the right to remain unmarried. If Vamilion had not come into her life, she would have probably eventually married Jonis and been a farmer's wife with half a dozen kids and a tired existence.

That thought made her weep for what might have been. Drake noticed her tears as they walked but said nothing and she hurriedly wiped them away. What would her life have been like with Vamilion instead? He would have loved her and she had no doubt she could easily come to love the King of Mountains back.

They would have had a heritage of magic and surely she would not have been as uncomfortable as the thought of being with Drake? Vamilion had Paget and she would always be Vamilion's first choice. But what would it have been like if fate had dealt Gailin a different hand? What if they had met when no hunter tracked him or he had no other love already in his life? Would they have grown to care for each other or would the magic make their attraction and bond instant?

Right now, considering how wretched she felt, Gailin would have gladly given up the magic and not be driven into either choice. Drake or Vamilion, neither was fair when magic manipulated the outcome. Why should she give up her free will in either case? Magic was to blame and she almost swore not to use it again if it were going to push her in a direction she didn't want to go. It was no better than what Drake had done to her, invoking name magic to force her to do this. Drake at least had a motive of a sort. Did she want children? She had not thought about it much. It seemed foolish to think about that before she had a man and with her grandmother as a responsibility, even that was beyond her.

Now Gailin had been launched into the world and was falling into a chasm with her life buried in mist. She might as well enjoy the flight. Maybe the beauty of small things was all she could expect. Having a child would be nice, despite the circumstances. Drake might be a decent husband for all she knew. Maybe she could keep him from harvesting more souls, for her sake. She would continue to let him tap into her magic and maybe that would enhance their relationship. She had no idea how this would come out but she would come to terms with it. A person dying of a slow growing tumor made much the same adjustment and while the diagnosis was grim, at least she was aware of her fate and would make the most of the time she had in her life.

Two days later they reached the town of Meeting on the eastern branches of the Lara River. Drake used name magic to forbid her to speak to anyone as they wandered in the streets of the relatively large town. He directed them to an inn where he purchased the nicest suite with money she didn't know he had. They took turns bathing and then he went down to ask the innkeeper where a priest could be found. While he was gone Gailin experimented with how much magic she could do despite his restrictions and found that other than calling to anyone mentally she seemed to be free to work. She conjured a clean set of clothes to get married in and then realized she had a worse problem. As soon as Drake walked back in the door, she presented it to him.

"Getting married is an oath. For a Wise One, taking an oath puts me into that royal clothing. The priest will notice."

Drake rocked back on his feet as he recognized this would interfere with his plans to remain behind the scenes, not known as a sorcerer. "I will just absorb him after the ceremony and he won't be able to tell anyone he has just seen magic," he suggested warily.

"No," she almost panicked, revolted that anyone would die because of her. "No, let me handle it. I...like you better when you aren't hurting others." It sounded incredibly awkward, but she had to say something to stop him if she weren't able to hinder him magically.

Drake looked at her oddly and then smirked as if this met his needs also. "Well, you make that possible. I haven't absorbed anyone since I met you. It's enough just to absorb you." He almost sounded glad that he hadn't found a need to kill someone either. They both privately thought it was a strange arrangement, but then he escorted her to the priest.

It was a simple ceremony with only the priest there and predictably, when Gailin's clothing shifted into the royal costume, she swiftly entered the priest's mind and stripped away the memory of the shock. Her intimate understanding of the human brain that she had gleaned allowed Gailin to tap into a minor portion of the mind and remove a memory. It was a practice that she intended to keep rare and hopefully use on Drake sometime soon. When the priest continued with the ceremony with only a moment's hesitation and then wandered back into his office without even congratulating the newlywed couple, Drake looked impressed.

"Subtle is better," Gailin commented and then turned back into her normal clothing and they left the little church. Now if only she could work a spell on herself to forget what else she was now bound to endure.

Chapter 12

Rumbling

Vamilion stood waist deep and filthy dirty in the ocean surf that swirled with noxious gasses and ash spewing from the volcano that now rose visibly above the surf in the bay at the mouth of the Laranian River. He had to speed up the eruption process when the first boat of sorcerers had arrived, leaving him no time, not even for daylight. Forcing the volcano's growth meant more powerful eruptions and he could not counter the tsunamis fast enough unless he stood right there in the water. The coastal villages would be wiped out otherwise and hopefully the volcano had encouraged evacuations already. So Vamilion grounded himself to the bedrock below him so he wasn't washed ashore every time the waves came, but that meant he also spent half the time underwater blackened to ink by the roiling ash and boiling gasses filling the surf. While he didn't technically need to breathe, it was a luxury Vamilion appreciated as he battled the minds of the sorcerers who knew he was there to challenge them.

Dozens of outlander sorcerers of the likes of Drake had come, commandeering a ship, and had tried to sneak in the mouth of the Laranian. Vamilion caught them before they reached fresh water and hit them with a tsunami from his convenient volcano, pulled them back out to sea and then dashed them onto the still steaming shore of the new piece of Land. Unfortunately killing sorcerers wasn't that easy. Their shattered ship washed all around Vamilion at his beachhead, but he would not allow these sorcerers even that much territory. He battered at their minds, hoping to break through but failed, though his attacks kept them busy.

Someone among them must have had a gift with weather or wind, for the clouds of ash began blowing in a perfectly unnatural direction, out to sea and rain clouds built up, washing the sky of ash that now fouled the waters Vamilion stood in. He probably looked like a monster made of lava, but he was not harmed in the least. Instead he countered by calling up great globs of still fresh magma to grow up over the legs of anyone standing on the island. The pain must have been excruciating for Vamilion heard their howls and some died, he sensed, buried in beds of freshly forming stone. The weather manipulating sorcerer fell to this fate and the magically manufactured storm clouds gave way to volcanic billowing once again.

However, some sorcerers escaped this tactic by changing themselves into something less human and slithering into the water or circling overhead like vultures, ready to swoop down the instant they spotted him. Perhaps being covered in ash and saltwater could be a benefit for Vamilion, for they could not see him in the night and vast blindness of the eruption. Again he forced the volcano to release more poison that rained down on the unnatural birds and the lava bombs fired like missiles down on anything that moved. Heaven help any of the villagers who lived nearby. They had been warned by the earthquakes and tsunamis before the invaders ever made their appearance but Vamilion could not afford to spare them his attention. And battle he did. By dawn he found himself with a glimmer of light lifting between the black water and the darker clouds formed from the new land mass.

With the sun's rise no minds came to challenge him. At last Vamilion let the volcano settle except for a crack of lava oozing on the island's northwest side, spewing out a perfect spot for a port in the deepest water near the island. It was the least he could do for the poor people who had to live in the shadow of an active volcano. He fully intended for this island he had made to be habitable and pleasant. As he wearily swam up and then climbed onto Gardway Island, as he christened it, Vamilion looked around and sensed no one dead or alive to battle. Wearily he walked the shoreline, strengthening the lava mixture beneath his feet. Any further eruptions out of the volcano hopefully would be meant for land building and not battling invaders. The volcano should probably cure for at least a year before anyone else touched this land and it would take that long to develop enough soil to support plant life. Vamilion would see to that and not speed up the process of bringing in greenery. He also made a few hot springs near the bay he had created and washed in them, enjoying being clean.

All this magic, however, left him no energy or thought to see how Gailin fared. Indeed, after three days in the dark of battle and blasts of ash, he could not think at all and fell asleep in one of his conjured hot springs. At dawn of the fourth day he thought to go tell Owailion about the battle he had encountered and almost forgot to go back to his tent up on the mountain to pack, or rather make all he had conjured disappear. And it was a good thing he did go, for he had left the tablet there unattended and the snows would have soon have buried it. Summer was fading and these mountains would soon be lost to the cold.

But then he picked up the tablet and absently looked over what Gailin had written. Then his hands began trembling. In an entire stream of consciousness, not a letter to him, she told him all she was enduring.

She had been trapped by the hunter when he discovered the map was a blank forgery. Drake had made it impossible for her to call for help or work magic to defend herself. When Vamilion read of the snake's ambition to get a magical heir, with Gailin as the mother, the volcano erupted again and he did nothing about the tidal wave that resulted. Over the several days' worth of writing Gailin obviously began to come to grips with her new reality and Vamilion began to calm into a more dangerous anger.

Owailion had done this. He had allowed her to go with the hunter out onto the plains where Vamilion could not follow. Instead of shadowing her as Vamilion would have done, Owailion had stayed down at the mouth of Don River building with his little toys and not checked on Gailin regularly to see that she would not be manipulated or harmed. Vamilion's anger seared and boiled, with responding earthquakes throughout the range on which he stood. But he forced himself to read to the end, holding down his gorge as Gailin dispassionately described her wedding night.

Why couldn't she have waited for him? Why had she walked into this danger? Why did Owailion allow this? Why didn't she just slip into the snake's mind and erase her name, slit his metaphorical throat and release the souls. Why hadn't Vamilion done that for her? Why had he abandoned his duty to the woman he already loved, despite himself? Why must she suffer this? Just like Owailion he would lose the companion that God had arranged for him and he would spend eternity alone with only memories of dying ladies for his solace. He might as well call down the avalanche of the ages over himself and be done with it.

Gailin's words cut off eventually, after describing the cold intimacy of the snake, leaving Vamilion with no idea exactly where she was or if she had survived. Drake might not kill her seeing as he wanted his magical heir, but perhaps Gailin had challenged him and he would have been forced to kill her. Vamilion didn't even know how long ago this had taken place. It had only been five days since he had read her last update, but that would not stop him now. He threw the tablet on the table and reached out his mind toward the north. Where was Gailin now? They had been heading for the Great Chain, but he couldn't hear her mind. Was Drake blocking her, shielding her from magical identification? Desperately Vamilion switched perspectives, not listening for her mind but instead using the mountains as his eyes. He had all the mountains there seeking for a beautiful lady traveling into the passes. They couldn't be hard to spot, but still, he saw nothing.

Vamilion could endure it no longer. He picked up the tablet and launched himself across the continent to another mountain nearest to Meeting. Illogically he hoped to see her without magic though it seemed foolish to expect that he could physically do what magic had been unable to accomplish. He looked the sky around, day and night. The clouds wheeled overhead, filled with the first snows that began to drift down before his misery and despair finally drove him to another tactic.

He would confront Owailion.

Using mountain to mountain, Vamilion launched himself to the southernmost point of the Great Chain, where the Don River emerged from a thousand cracks among the peaks. He stood at the last high ridge with a Wise One's palace visible below him down on the plains below near the roaring Don River, just above a waterfall. Owailion had forbidden him from changing the geology but right at that moment, Vamilion didn't care what the elder Wise One wanted. He wanted answers.

Vamilion lifted his hand out over the valley that stretched before him. With a thought, he dammed up the river with a well-placed avalanche of rubble. Snapping trees and crushed rocks filled the river's path and blocked up the channel. The flow began to back up, forming a lake and the old path failed. The waterfall dropped to a trickle in the lower river and Vamilion smiled at the bare cliff that had been revealed, now devoid of the roaring veil of the falls.

Next Vamilion felt for the fault beneath him that had formed the long Great Chain of mountains like jewels on a necklace. That fault stopped here, blocking him from traveling farther south. So what if Owailion said not to make more mountains, he thought rebelliously. Vamilion reached deeper into the fault and with the force of his anger, he cracked the earth to its roots. He wasn't seeking a volcano, but uplift. His hand rose and with it, the eastern half of the widened crack he had created. Below him the land pitched and screamed. If there were not a magical foundation under that Wise One's palace, it would have toppled. The lake he was forming deep in the mountains behind his landfall became rivers in new directions and found a way around his dam, gushing back into the Don.

What would have taken a million years took a matter of hours but Vamilion had a new mountain and river before his eyes. Then, as if he were not troubled by his own rebellion, he leapt to his newly created peak and began another mountain in the chain, another jewel in the Land's necklace. He would surround the entire continent in his creations if Owailion did not come to him and explain himself and help him find Gailin. The pitching earth and snapping of solid stone did not trouble him. The loss of the Queen, that hurt beyond words.

"Gilead, stop!" Owailion's words echoed as he appeared behind Vamilion on the newly created peak. The King of Creating looked placid and hardly surprised at what his younger protégé had done to gain his attention. However, he also didn't look pleased; more annoyed that he had been pulled away from his project. Owailion stripped off work gloves and stuffed them in the pockets of his welding apron with a huff.

Vamilion turned around slowly lest he slide on the unstable mountain top. Having name magic invoked on him only angered him more, but his inherent patience allowed Vamilion to turn to face the man he needed now to help him find Gailin. Owailion's haphazard, lazy look, even as he balanced precariously on the top of the world must have been meant to put Vamilion over the top, encouraging him to explode like a volcano. It wouldn't work just yet.

"You shouldn't do that, Owailion. We are equals and I don't know your name. Right now that might be a good thing or I might just kill you. The Queen is missing because you let her go off with that snake. This is what she wrote to me; the last I've heard from her. I cannot find her mind anywhere and the mountains have not seen her. I want to know what you've been doing to protect her." He held out the tablet.

Owailion took the slab without looking away from his colleague, as if he now began to understand something; no matter that he had never set eyes on Gailin, Vamilion was already bonded to her. His profound anger witnessed to that. It took a moment before the King of Creating dare look down at the words Gailin had written. Owailion's usually sour face changed little. Maybe a pursed lip or a breath released just a little more slowly as he absorbed what had happened, but Vamilion watched him intently, waiting for the impact of some regret on the man's frosty façade.

When he had finished reading Owailion looked up toward the northwest, perhaps duplicating the search that Vamilion had tried earlier, seeking for one mind across a vast expanse and hearing nothing. Then slowly he looked back at his companion just a few feet away.

"Erase it," he ordered and handed the tablet back.

Vamilion shook his head, refusing to do as ordered, not even taking the tablet. He would not brush away her words any more than he would brush away her life as Owailion seemed to have done. Then, to his horror, Owailion did it for him, smashing the slab

162

against the rough mountain top. The stone slate shattered into chunks and then Owailion crushed the shattered pieces with a thought and let it crumble to dust under his boots.

Vamilion suddenly wanted to do the same to Owailion's bones but even more, he wanted an explanation.

Owailion finally spoke. "You might not understand it now... or ever, but this is what is meant to happen. She is coming into her power. He will not kill her. Nor will he ever sway her heart. Trust that."

"No," Vamilion replied flatly. "Where is she?"

Owailion looked down at the rubble sliding over the sheer slopes on which he balanced under the pulsing anger of the King of the Mountains. Then the King of Creating looked back up and flatly said the words to ignite an inferno.

"I will not tell you."

Vamilion's anger blasted out at his peer before either could even consider it. No logic remained within. And Owailion's refusal to give a simple answer seemed so arbitrary and ridiculous he had no desire to reason it out. Vamilion's Wise One instincts fled in the face of simple human rage. Was that what Owailion wanted? Well, he would have it.

The earth shook and both men slid down, on separate sides of the sheer ridge of the newly cut peak. Instinctively Vamilion made his pick appear out of thin air and slammed it into the rock face as he fell, but the magic of the Talisman was to break and the fifty feet of stone above him began to crumble free.

With a mental shove he pushed the weight of it the other way, toward the direction Owailion was falling and it crumbled like a stone rain down the northern side. For his part, Owailion didn't take the attack lightly. A storm formed overhead as Vamilion struggled to remain on the cliff face and lightning struck at him before he could recover, blasting him free. Desperately Vamilion launched his thoughts to another mountain, on the far side of the continent and shifted there.

Exhausted and bitterly cold, Vamilion caught his breath and then threw a powerful wave of sheer magic at Owailion, hoping it would hit him off the mountain far away, but the wave missed when Owailion disappeared. The attack collided violently with the peak, leaving Vamilion rattled with the mountain's pain, and he lost trace of his opponent in the stony carnage. The King of the Mountains felt ill at ease hiding, but he didn't know where the next attack would come, so he kept flipping from one locale to another and the storm clouds and lightning followed him through every jump. He next hid in one of the deeper mines where iron had been discovered instead of the diamonds hoped for and the men had abandoned the dig. Instead he found new miners there and blended in with them for a few hours. It gave Vamilion time to think about what had happened.

For one thing, Owailion had known this would put him over the edge, Vamilion thought, demanding a battle. Wise Ones were not to lose their temper. The magic required them to be decent, kind people and being driven to the intensity of a full on brawl required quite a trigger. And Owailion had wanted a fight. Why? What was he trying to prove? Was murder the intent? More like suicide. Neither one of them could kill the other... well that wasn't true. The only way to kill a Seated Wise One was to command them to die. Since he did not know Owailion's true name it was impossible to use that means to kill him, but that didn't stop Owailion from doing the same to him. And yet he hadn't done that. He had only driven him to a murderous rage. If the King of Creation was trying to commit suicide this seemed like an insane way of going about it.

But still they threw blows at each other from a distance, refusing to speak to each other and explain what was going on. They might end up wrecking the world, but they would still be alive, standing in the middle of the ruins. Not very wise of Wise Ones. Most of all Vamilion simply wanted an answer: Where was Gailin and why would Owailion allow her to be used so horribly?

He tried to locate his enemy again somewhere in the Land but the very act of reaching for him alerted Owailion of his location. In a panic Vamilion shouted about a cave-in and got his fellow miners running out of the tunnels. Owailion's blow hit and the men all scrambled out of the entrance in panic and then stared in wonder at Vamilion. Several of these men recognized him from other times he had been about the mines, but now they started to look on him as a savior – the patron saint of miners all over the world. Vamilion was abashed but when another blow came and lightening hit the rock face above the mine's opening, he abruptly disappeared rather than draw more danger down on the men and that did not help their impression of him.

Next Vamilion took refuge on his new island, Gardway. Perhaps Owailion had not discovered the new addition to the map and the thundering from the still active volcano would mask the rumbling thoughts Vamilion still harbored. He rested and re-covered in the hot springs again but he also worried about being parboiled with a well-placed lightning bolt and so didn't stay long. Finally after three days of exhaustive fighting Vamilion went back to his newest mountain and waited for Owailion to find him there. Hopefully they could finish their discussion and do something to help Gailin.

It wasn't to be. Owailion, with his gift of traveling instantly, didn't have to appear to do his magic. In-stead Vamilion felt himself plucked up off the moun-taintop and thrown violently through the air. He hardly had time to think before he was slammed in the middle of the plains, hundreds of miles from the nearest mountain. There Owailion dropped him like a load of stone. The landing crumpled the ground underneath Vamilion and he lost consciousness for a time. And when he came to painfully, he wept in exhaustion and frustration. He would either have to make himself wretchedly sick or start walking to leave this place. And overhead, Owailion's thunder-storms waited.

Vamilion lay on his back, aching everywhere and stared up into the pensive storm. It occurred to him then that he could just lay there and refused to fight any more. He would just have to turn himself into a pile of stone here, a cairn in the grasses before he found his answers. And so that is what he did. A pile of stones in the middle of the winter's dying grasses replaced his body and Vamilion went to sleep, maybe forever.

Chapter 13

Secret Rebellions

Drake insisted they keep moving, regardless of the fact that in Meeting they had returned to the ley lines, fall had descended and the mountains he feared remained ahead. Gailin had to go along with it, even though she found it hard to do anything at that point. She almost crumbled in on herself, with her magic the only thing that remained to remind her that she was human and not an object. She obeyed Drake's instructions to head north, following the appropriate branch in the Laranian River, but a slave had more freedoms and liveliness. She couldn't help herself much of the time and as they reached the mountains, moving away from most of the villages, she grew more despondent. She lost hope that maybe in the Great Chain the King of Mountains would find her. As they hid themselves among the passes Drake kept them invisible and her miserable.

It didn't help that Drake insisted on trying for the baby every night and she vomited every time afterwards. The reptilian memories and his constant draining touch revolted her. Drake took this as a good sign, suspecting morning sickness but she knew better. He nauseated her and she couldn't stand the smell of him, or get the feel of him off her body. She washed in the river almost frantically and wept there in the water with grief for her own essence. She wasn't Gailin any longer.

Oh, she knew there were girls everywhere who ended up in loveless marriages or found themselves sold off by their fathers as part of a business deal, but she never thought she would end up that way. She had originally rejected Jonis because of that prospect; marriage out of duty, not love. But this was different. She once upon a time imagined that with magic she could do anything, and held onto the hope that a foreordained lover awaited her. Vamilion, her knight in shining armor, was going to come and rescue her just as soon as Paget died, or when he found a way to kill Drake. But Vamilion never came.

And as the days stretched into weeks her resentment of magic grew with every step. At first she directed her anger and disgust inward and then recognized that led to dangerous depression. The tales of the Queen of Rivers echoed in Gailin's dreams at night. Part of her quietly considered using name magic on herself to escape this misery. That led to instability in her magic, she discovered. She couldn't conjure much accurately. Since their survival relied on her ability to provide food, clothing and shelter as the wet weather descended, this attitude grew dangerous. She also couldn't bear to listen into Drake's thoughts so when he grew volatile, she wasn't forewarned or prepared and instead of diffusing his lusts for death, she almost gave into ignoring them. She could tune out his dreadful thoughts as long as he didn't act on them. If he spoke aloud about going after another soul, she would say something, but otherwise she wouldn't rouse herself to object. And she had almost forgotten about the souls he had taken. She couldn't go into his mind at night now because of his prohibition against using magic on him, but when she forgot about the souls she needed to rescue, that should have been alarming. Yet, it wasn't.

Rather than falling into the inward depression, Gailin began focusing her unrest and anger outward; toward Owailion, someone she had not met but one she could truly blame for her predicament. It had not been Vamilion who had suggested that she respond to Drake's amorous advances, but Owailion. He was the one who wanted her to lure Drake away from the ley lines. Something else must have happened to Vamilion, she convinced herself. He would not have left her in Drake's clammy grasp. If he knew, the King of the Mountains surely would have written to her. He would have read the book, seen her despondency and sent a message back or found a way to show her that she was still in his thoughts. Owailion must have blocked him or found a way to keep Vamilion from coming to her rescue.

Her single bright light was her healing. Whenever they came into a village Drake allowed her to find the healer in town and offer her services. She could not speak of magic to whomever she met, and she held no hope of sending out a message, but it lifted her spirits. And in one village the ancient woman who acted as the village healer spoke to her gently about an apothecary who lived up by a huge lake called Ameloni on the other side of the mountains and suggested that she should go there to replenish her supplies of herbs. Drake wasn't aware of this little conversation and so when she kept walking north, even when the river petered out in the pass, and led the way over to the far side, he didn't object.

Lake Ameloni filled the plains on the far side of the mountain pass and the first snow descended just in time to encourage them to find this vaunted apothecary. A single cabin near the shore and the remains of an herb garden outside told her she might be in the correct place, but Gailin dared greatly and pressed her mind forward to see what kind of person she was going to encounter. A gentleman, alone but not lonely, met her thoughts and with relief she could magically smell a wide range of spices, herbs and other plants in his cabin. This was the apothecary she had hoped to meet.

"No speaking, Gailin. No magic," Drake warned, for he rarely let her speak with anyone on the off chance it might be someone who knew magic. She had long ago given up fighting the name magic imposed on her and simply nodded. Really she was just curious and that part of being a Wise One had not died with every other part of her. Being a healer, wanting to learn more and trying to expand beyond the limits of her marriage to Drake gave her hope.

It was only mid-afternoon but the sun was already lowering when Drake knocked on the door of the apothecary. It took a long while for the man to reach the door and Gailin sensed he had to come from the basement where he had a still room, cool year round for the storage of his wares. When he came to the door, the gentleman looked surprised. An older gentleman with graying hair and huge hands, he seemed a simple, roughhewn person who looked like he saw perhaps five people a year given the rustic, hard to reach location. His beard, untrimmed, and his leather clothes witnessed to his rough lifestyle. He wore a leather apron, work gloves and a startled look, but greeted them well enough.

"Oh, I was expecting a hunter," he said cheerfully. "How may I help you?"

"Are you the Apothecary?" Drake prefaced. "We heard about you in one of the villages down on the other side of the pass."

"Yes," he nodded, giving Gailin a strange look, for she kept her head down, humbly standing behind her husband, not daring to make eye contact. "I provide herbs and such things in this area. Are you in need something?"

"My wife here has an interest. We're traveling and need to replenish her supplies," Drake replied.

The Apothecary invited them into his home which seemed completely devoted to his work. The table, the hearth, all flat surfaces and even his bed tucked into a corner, were covered with bottles, leaves, bowls and powders of his trade. The haphazard and overwhelming display of medicinal wealth made Gailin's eyes go wide.

"Tell the man what we need," Drake ordered and she started. The Apothecary looked at her, still concerned, though he recovered well enough by finding a scrap of leather and a charred piece of wood with which to write. He swept aside an empty mortar and pestle to make a writing surface and looked up, prepared to make a list.

A light went off at last in Gailin's mind. She could treat herself for her depression. The things she needed would also be a warning to this man if he knew something about the herbs and supplements he sold. "I need dried spinach, fish oil, hypericum..."

Dutifully the Apothecary wrote all these items down, nodding his understanding. When she added a few things they legitimately needed, like ginger and garlic, he looked up and she peered at him face on, showing him that she wasn't necessarily cowed by her husband and that she at one time had a mind of her own.

"Well, it will take a bit to get this together, but I have it all here somewhere," the Apothecary muttered. "Can you wait here for a while?"

Without pausing for the answer, the Apothecary went down into his basement still room and left

Gailin and Drake upstairs in the chaos. Without asking permission she began visibly sorting through what she saw and in wonder recognized how a little organizing would truly display what this man had. She had never seen such a vast array of healing needs. She found bottles and corks, mortar and pestle, dried leaves of all variety flung about the room haphazardly and couldn't resist. She began organizing.

She bundled like leaves together and found twine in the windowsill to tie them in a bunch. She gathered empty bottles and began pouring the ground powders into them. One sniff or a brief taste told her exactly which medicinal herb she encountered and she looked around for the apothecary's labeling system. None seemed in evidence so she looked back at Drake. He wouldn't object with her helping as long as magic wasn't in evidence. She took out her book and stylus and began cutting one page into little strips of paper.

Drake looked disgusted and bored. He had not wanted to come here, but he nodded his approval when her labor managed to clear the only chair in the place and he was able to sit. He didn't bother offering to help and instead cleaned his nails with his belt knife, paying little attention to her actions. Could she get a message to the apothecary? It would not require magic and she wasn't 'calling' to anyone. Carefully, on the bottle of caraway seeds she was labeling she wrote a second word. "Help." On the next she wrote "Queen of Healing" instead of the words that belonged there. On the next she wrote "Name Magic" and then reconsidered. A simple apothecary would know nothing about magic or her situation. Yet something subversive awoke in her and she ended up labeling every bottle there with a message to someone. She only had to hope that Drake had been honest when he said he could not read the language of the Land.

When she heard the apothecary stomping back up the ladder from his still room, she paused. The old man lifted the floor hatch and gasped. She had managed to work her way through fully half the room and made his bed livable along with the chair and part of the table. Awkwardly she finished writing on one final label, tied it to the cork and then put the bottle on his mantle where she had been storing her newly organized medicines. Without looking at the Apothecary's stunned face Gailin gathered the now empty bowls, put them in his wash tub and then turned toward him.

"You're a god-send," the Apothecary commented with a chuckle. Even though he had his hands full of their purchases he began exploring her labeling system and handiwork. Gailin watched the old man read one label and freeze a bit as her true message came through to him. Instead of cinnamon like she should have put on the jar she had put 'tell someone'. The Apothecary moved on to the next bottle and read there, getting the point quite quickly.

Then he turned back to his customers as if there was nothing amiss in his bottles. "This is wonderful. If you can stay, I'll give you these for free and you

can finish the job. The still room is worse, trust me."
Then he set down all the little bags and few bottles
of liquid items he had prepared for them.

Gailin didn't dare look over at Drake, for then he
would know she wanted to remain behind in this
wondrous place, exploring the herbs and leaving her
little messages. She looked down at her hands and
commanded them not to tremble. She had finally broken free a little and the prospect of more crafted a
rage against the name magic she could not contain.
Oh, to be able to speak.

Drake spoke for her. "No, we must be going. How
much do we owe you?" Then to put emphasis on his
decision, Drake added privately to her alone. "I'm
hungry enough to kill him, Gailin, so don't make a
scene."

Carefully she nodded and did not look up.

"You don't owe me a thing, sir. Your wife here has
done more than pay for the medicines. And if you'll
let me, I have one more thing for you." The Apothecary found a leather pouch in the mess Gailin had
not reached yet and swept their purchases into the
bag and then he added a small mortar and pestle that
he put directly into Gailin's hands. She looked down
into the stone bowl and found something else in the
bottom of it. She didn't dare react or look closely to
see what he had added. There would be time later.

The Apothecary saw them to the door and off with
a wave, a smile and an invitation to return any time
they were near Lake Ameloni. And as they walked
off into the twilight, Gailin made a show of putting

their newly acquired medicines into her bag. Then she was finally able to feel what he had given her inside the mortar.

A little pendent, silver and pearl, with a stylized lily carved into the metal. With an effort Gailin resisted the temptation to look closely at it, but she now realized she had found something she didn't think she would be capable of while in the chains of Drake's name magic; a pendent, the key to opening her palace, given to her by her future doorkeeper.

Gailin smiled in secret rebellion and followed after her husband back over the pass and into the mountains.

* * *

Two months later Gailin looked at the palace and could not breathe. It gleamed in the setting winter sun, setting off the white marble walls carved with graceful bas relief scenes of forests and lilies. The stained glass windows and the snow blinded her in gold and lavender light. She wished passionately that she could see this place in the summer, with rich gardens not buried under snow or the chill of winter closing in on her, but nonetheless, she knew her home. Privately she tried not to seem enchanted, but for Drake's sake she said nothing and kept her eyes on the building itself.

"What's it doing here in the middle of this tight little valley? It's indefensible," Drake commented from behind her as they hiked down out of the pass.

"Not everything is about war or defense," Gailin commented, letting him pass her by so that she could continue to admire the sight. Also, she feared lest her newly acquired pendent would really open the place even though she had not completed her Seeking tasks. "This place is far enough away from people to be at peace no matter what happens in the rest of the world. It was not meant to be a fortress but an oasis."

Her husband groused privately at that comment, but he didn't object to the idea of staying in a warm hall that night since they had been climbing into the mountains for two months now and it made him edgy. This was the mountain man's territory and he felt exposed especially with the surrounding mountain walls, despite his renewed access to ley lines. The invisibility spell Drake maintained on their movements took a lot of energy and while the place bristled with power and he had Gailin to sustain him, Drake couldn't help but think the mountains were watching him.

"So, can we get in?" Drake asked. But just as he said the words he plowed face first into an invisible wall fifty feet from the actual wall of the palace, about where the land leveled out and the snow buried gardens began. "Damn, it's like before, when the Land was sealed. Why is it sealed to you if this is your palace?"

Gailin stepped up to the seal and placed her hand gently against the invisible barrier. It wasn't opened to her yet, she realized with relief. She would find a way to keep Drake out of her palace even if it meant

never entering it herself. While she was just specu-
lating, she had to answer something. "I told you, as
a Wise One there are certain duties and skills I must
learn before I can take my place here."

Drake's inherent impatience expressed itself in a
huff. "It seems a waste. You aren't rulers and you
hardly use the magic you've got. Why the fancy
clothing and royal homes if you aren't truly act-
ing like a queen? And they won't even let you
in... whoever 'they' are?"

Gailin looked over at her husband with a mixture of pity and resignation. She had often tried to
at least explain what she understood of her duties
and the ethical bounds of being a Wise One but they
seemed like nothing but hurdles to Drake, meant to
be knocked down or ignored. On their trip up into
the mountains twice more she had felt the compulsion to go help someone they passed in the villages
that lined the river and while he had not forbidden
her to help, Drake had also watched her healing with
deep suspicion. She had cured a rampant fever with
a touch and had helped lessen the terrible scarring of
a child who had fallen in a fire. She actively used her
gift of magic as well as her knowledge of the important herbs and medicines to do her work and everyone who witnessed her healing acknowledged it was
magic. And there had not been a peep about hanging
a witch this time. Drake had not commented but later
he expressed disappointment.

"Too bad you cannot do that to yourself," he had
muttered, not really meaning to be overheard, but he

was anyway. The fact that she had not yet come up pregnant rankled at him and he was growing increasingly impatient. Since they were following her instincts into the mountains with deep winter coming on, he had hoped to find someplace warm to really work on that aspect of his plan.

"I don't know why we have the grand palaces," Gailin replied to the long forgotten comment. "I assume so it impresses people like you. You didn't trust me until I wore that fancy clothing. Others like you, seeing a Wise One in the palace, might take our magic a bit more seriously."

"Not if it weren't on the ley lines. There are three that pass within twenty miles of here, did you know?"

"No," she reminded him, "I don't feel them.

"Well, I do and they have made this a wonderful place to build a cabin and winter over. This will do." Drake dropped his bag and from the set in his body, she knew he intended to remain, no matter what compulsion she felt, which meant she had to stay there with him. With a sigh Gailin set down her own bag and pushed up the sleeves of her coat. Despite wanting to keep some of her abilities secret, she had finally admitted to Drake that she could conjure far more than water or they would have starved. Conjuring allowed them to feed themselves in these cold mountains and their warmer clothing had been enough to impress Drake, who didn't seem to be able to bring more than the simple things into being. He dealt with fire, wind and simple, one element items like a dagger of steel and such. It was her responsibility to create food and shelter every night. Now it seemed he had no intention of moving on from this magically rich valley until spring arrived.

Unwillingly Gailin swept snow away from the ground in a square large enough to build a little cabin. River stones began to lift out of the frozen earth and stacked themselves into a foundation off the ground and then planks and walls began forming. She hated to add anything to this perfect place but she knew she would be commanded if she didn't do it willingly.

While she worked Drake watched her with possessive glee. She didn't fight him much outwardly when it came to magic; he still used her name daily to reinforce the original commands he had given her, but she also remained silent with most of his other desires. He wanted that son and she was forced to let him try. Other than that there was little to discuss and he preferred to ignore her as he would a horse or his boots; necessary and useful but little else. This meant she wasn't obliged to explain other things to him like compulsions, Talismans or Vamilion and the book. Those things she still kept close to her heart in hopes that something would change. Now that she had a little hope that the Apothecary would get out her message, she found silence easier to bear.

Somewhere within she might have lost hope for a while. Surely Vamilion was looking for her now but there was nothing new in the book and no sign that anyone wanted to find her. This pained her but for all she knew the invasion of which Vamilion spoke had come and he had other duties. She looked daily and wrote often of her thoughts when she had the chance, but Drake demanded to see what she wrote often. The book that she had used as an anatomy text and to record her observations in herbs had now become a journal as well. She used an invisibility spell over quite a bit that she wrote but always had something innocuous to show Drake if he snatched it out of her hands unexpectedly. His impatience drove him to snap at inopportune times. Was he hoping for news from these invaders and hadn't heard? Well, then they both were hoping for someone that was not coming.

Because it was obvious she wasn't going to get pregnant instantly, Drake had insisted that they keep moving, wearing themselves out and living on the very edge of settled areas, as if he were afraid to be discovered. And he demanded an explanation as to why she was not yet pregnant.

"I don't know why," she replied frankly. "I haven't studied the female body in much detail like we studied a male in the summer. It didn't come up and..."

He cut her off with a threat. "Then I'll have to get a female body to examine and you'll find out what is wrong with you."

Half a dozen rude comments flashed through Gailin's mind, safely behind her shields, not passing her lips. Instead she spoke with a measured tone, dangerous and threatening. "If you kill some poor woman to bring me a body, I swear it won't help you understand or get you your son." To emphasize her point, that oath put her into her stunning regalia, complete with a warm white fur cloak to compliment the frigid weather. "Name magic can't 'order' me to understand what I don't want to understand."

Drake had to consider her words for a few hours before he dropped the subject, though he never admitted she was right. Fortunately they had already left the more populated areas at the foot of the mountains and women of child bearing age were few. If he did manage to find someone already dead, Gailin would have kept her promise if only to hinder him. She wasn't the one who wanted children and at this point the thought of bringing a child into this toxic and dangerous relationship seemed foolhardy. With every prayer for her own rescue she also yearned to not become pregnant. She knew of herbs that would prevent it but she couldn't manage to break the compulsion enough to put them in a tea for herself. He had commanded her to bear him a child. Perhaps prayers were just as effective as herbs. Every month, when her cycle came she smiled privately and hoped her luck would hold.

Now winter in her magic-crafted cabin strung along eternally. Cooped up with Drake, with nothing to do but feel the endless tension of his impatience nearly drove her insane. The constant, glorious reminder that was her castle stood like the marble tombstone of a giant right outside her door. She wanted to leave – go on walks in the snow, explore the valley, learn the plants of the area, climb a mountain just to see something new, but any time she suggested it or tried to leave, Drake wanted to try again for the baby. The days became weeks, and then months and the snow only grew deeper. To show her restlessness and just to irritate him, Gailin knitted baby things out of conjured wool she spun in her fingers. For his part Drake whittled spikes that he drove into the snow like hidden traps. Winter felt like it would never end.

Then one night she had another momentous dream. It fell like the rain that would melt the pervasive snow in her mind and wash everything away. She felt clean again after months of Drake's clammy hands about her neck and she wanted to hold onto it. In her dream she stood on the stoop of the cabin looking up onto the night toward the mountain tops, not daring to take the step down to the ground for Drake would call her back. Instead she reached for the invisible bag she kept over her shoulder where she hid her book, the candle that had no purpose, the pendant and the Heart Stone. For some reason her hand found the candle and brought it out. With a thought she lit it magically and then held it high against the winter stars. She didn't know why but her desire to see that candle and know its purpose now became a magical compulsion. She whispered one thing into the night.

"Crack the lines."

Chapter 14

Broken Body, Empty Mind

Waking might be a poor word for what made the cairn crack. Ideas drove into the stone of Vamilion's mind and began to melt the frost on his bones, but he became aware. And these ideas had not come from long rumination, for he had been unaware during his hibernation. For all he knew Owailion still lingered outside the stones ready to blast him to rubble, but these ideas came and harried him until he relented and began thinking.

Gailin – you know her name. You never swore not to use her name that way. It's wrong to have such absolute control over someone, but is there not a time to use it? Owailion used it on you. Does that justify it? Vamilion's second idea stemmed from that. You don't want to call her because it might be perceived as need, but at least hear from her. You have not used the tablet. You destroyed it in your misery and anger. You're a fool, but maybe you can reestablish the connection to the book and you can learn where she is that way.

Then he remembered the last time he had read a message from her book, before she had been taken. She had been so excited about finding that blasted map with its ley lines. That memory stunned him, for he had not even recalled something she had mentioned. Gailin had written it only in passing – about the ley line map and how it might be possible to crack the ley lines back into the earth and strip any magic of these invaders that relied on shallow ley line magic. Why hadn't he thought of that?

Because you're a fool, he again told himself. You let your worry and anger at being manipulated overwhelm your common sense. Owailion arranged for Gailin to be manipulated on purpose and you wanted only to figure out why she had disappeared instead of relying on your bond with her. Just because you know Owailion better and wanted to understand him, you ignored all you could have learned from her. Call her.

If I call her, I'll see her. The bond will become a compulsion. You won't be able to escape loving her, he warned himself. You are still being a fool, he thought next. The bond is already addling your mind. You need her to be safe and that is the first and only priority. So the misery of a split heart lasts twenty years longer. What of it. You're going to have to look her in the eye eventually. Now is better. What about Paget? What will she think?

"Forget her, you fool," Owailion's mind voice rumbled through, interrupting Vamilion's scattered thoughts. Had the King of Creating hovered there just outside of the cairn's range for months, waiting for his reawakening to give him that familiar message?

"Stay away from me unless you have something worthwhile to say," Vamilion shot back and then blocked further interruption. He wanted to think for himself, but he hated it when Owailion was right. He needed to forget Paget's feelings for the moment and work on helping Gailin. And that meant calling her with name magic.

Without any real idea how it would work, Vamilion shook the petrifaction from his eyes and found he could see the sky though he hadn't managed to move yet. The scent of spring had come to the plains and he wanted to consider the clouds and the warmth that began slowly to creep into his cairn. Then, with a tremendous effort he tried to move. And he discovered he couldn't.

The pain rippled through his body like an avalanche of stone had hit him all at once and buried him again. Within the agony Vamilion managed to master the magic to become completely human again and then tried to move his legs. Nothing worked. He could move his arms a little and tried to leverage himself up but a second wave of torture rolled down his spine and he collapsed again. A little below his chest he found nothing worked. He could feel a little but that could be his imagination. Was he paralyzed? Had he been so damaged by that fall? The thought horrified him. He knew as a Seated King he could not die, but nothing in the Wise One ethos said anything about living an eternity as an invalid. Vamilion let the torment echo across the valley of his mind while this thought crashed onto him. Then, without willing it he turned these incredible pangs into something else. He felt the earth begin quaking underneath him.

The pressure to rise began to shake the ground and Vamilion forced his mind down into the bowels of the earth straining for something to snap into place. An earthquake rippled through his back, with the two pieces pressing and straining against each other, about to move with devastating consequences. He felt the rotation of the earth as the clouds passed heedlessly overhead. His breath formed into wind and his fingers reached into the stone and bedrock. He felt the molten core of the earth underneath and then with a roar, he tore the earth open.

Crack the ley lines? He imagined them like rivers flowing over bare stone, past seams and crevices, but tied to the bedrock on which it relied. He expanded his mind to the edges of the Land; to Jonjonel in the northwest, to Tamaar in the southwest, to the nameless lake of fog in the far northeast and the Don Forest in the southeast. He sensed the great pan of the plate on which his mountains grew. They were the diamonds about the graceful neck of the Land and he knew her intimately. And he would break her. Like an egg cracking open, he squeezed, feeling the magma ooze through his fingers. The rock wailed in protest. Hundreds of earthquakes shook the villages and great cracks appeared above ground, swallowing the remaining winter snows. The sea pulled away from the coasts and then washed in, filling the marshy deltas with salt and killing the soil there.

But the blue light of magic that flowed and tempted outlander magicians sank into the cracks he created. His magic had altered the stone so profoundly that power clung, clambering to stay on the bedrock. Vamilion did not listen to its voice. He poured ley magic like ice down on the hot coals of the beating heart of the world where it steamed instantly, joined the core and became something to feed the well magic of the Wise Ones. Basking in the well magic's heat, his mind stretched back over his domain, seeking anywhere the magic had flowed and found nothing. It all had been cracked open and spilled, the lifeblood of evil magic. Outlanders would have to bring their own power in order to work their spells here ever after. Then Vamilion ponderously sealed up the cracks and healed scars of his tearing hands, smoothing the stones again, leaving the Land to reverberate like a bell a while longer until it grew still and recovered.

As he came back into awareness of his abused body, Vamilion heard his breathing had grown shallow. He doubted he would retain consciousness. The agony of the Land from such wrenching had traveled down his back and he felt for a bit as if he had come unhinged. The buzzing in his ears sounded like hissing steam escaping a long forgotten vent and the clouds closed in from the sides, growing dim. But he had one more act of magic left before he gave into the cairn again.

"Gailin, come to me." Had he said that aloud? Could he say it in magic? He didn't know, nor would he be alive enough to know if he had succeeded. He just knew he tried.

* * *

At dawn Gailin stood on the stoop as she had in her dream, curious to see if it had been real. The snow had begun to melt and the mountains, heavy with it seemed to sigh, but nothing changed to tell her that this dream bore remembering. Experimentally she reached behind herself to bring forth the candle and reenact the events of the dream. She looked at the hunk of wax, wondering why she still even carried the thing. She had never used it, lit it or shown it to Drake. Had she even written about it in the book so Vamilion knew she had found one of her Talismans? She could not remember. Surely he would have said something if she had.

Before she could light the taper, however, the rumbling started. A sudden, unexpected jolt threw Gailin against the doorway and she looked up at the snow hanging from the slopes surrounding their valley. With an earthquake an avalanche would come down and completely swallow their poor little cabin. Frantically, she rushed in and reached for Drake to rouse him from bed, but the floor lurched beneath her and coals from the fire fell off the hearth and skittered past her, lighting the linens on the bed. Drake sat up in alarm and made his own judgment of the rumbling he heard. He reached out toward her, mouth open, about to say something deadly when she saw his eyes roll back in his head and he fell back against the pillows. Gailin crawled to the bed rather than be knocked back down as she heard the crashing of trees above the cabin and felt a sudden rush as air was displaced. Some alarming instinct made her grasp Drake's hand and with the other she held the candle high. She knew to her core where she wanted to go as the avalanche hit the cabin wall and a wave of white met her vision.

She closed her eyes and wished.

Peace didn't come with her wish. She felt the ground still pitching beneath her, but the cabin and the white had disappeared. Instead she held Drake's hand, kneeling in the new spring grasses just outside her old home by the village where she had been born. She knelt in her nightgown, beside Drake's unconscious body that apparently she had taken with her, moving from one earthquake storm to another. The trees in the forest danced like reeds in a pond during a wind storm. She dare not stand up so she dropped the candle and crawled a few feet closer to her husband. Unaccountably the candle disappeared but she wasn't concerned about that.

Instead Gailin lifted Drake's lids and saw he was unconscious. His breathing grew so shallow she could not count how many he took with the jouncing of the earth knocking it out of him. She felt for his heartbeat at his neck and felt a fluttering, like it tripped fifty times in an effort to bring about one single decent beat. Again on instinct she placed her hand on his heart and then with a magical pulse, jarred his heart. This seemed to help, for she felt it take on a much more normal beat; painfully slow, but regular. What had happened to him?

What was happening to Drake and the whole world? The earthquakes continued to rock and while she felt safe enough out of doors and away from the trees, these tremblers continued for ages. The ocean-like waves passed through the plains right in front of her terrifyingly close. Until it settled, she would not bring Drake into the house, even if that meant treating him right there on the grasses in front of the cabin. At least this far south it was warmer and spring had come.

This led her to think about how she had arrived a thousand miles away instantly. She looked for the candle and found it again in the invisible pack she carried at her back and she was grateful that it was always with her. The most precious possessions she owned, all invisibly hidden had come with her in their hurried, magical escape. And the candle had been the key. Magical travel must be the gift of the Talisman. She again held the candle out in front of her and thought of where else she could go with it and nothing came to mind. She wouldn't return to the palace in the mountains until the trembling ended and the only other place she had been that she wanted to remember was here.

And despite herself, she had to stay with Drake. Curiosity drew her back and she put away the candle to look into what she could do to free herself while given this time of peace in the middle of this geologic chaos. What had done this to Drake? Since his unconsciousness happened almost simultaneously, she assumed it was related to the tremendous geological changes the Land endured right now. Experimentally Gailin delved into Drake's mind to see how that fared and was staggered, first that she could enter it once again, for he had blocked her actively except at night when he held her by the throat, feeding on her. Now the crumbling walls of his mind were gone and instead a vast open plain of ash spread out before her mind's eye. No walls or even stones to trip upon marred the dusty terrain. The only thing to interrupt the metaphorical plains of Drake's mind was the arch of souls, now not lined with stone, but with a blue light that seemed to stretch the membrane across the void that she had not been able to touch since Drake had made his mandate that she not be able to do magic against him.

But things had changed. He was unconscious and the earth was splitting in two. Could she cut free the trapped souls now? Experimentally Gailin conjured a knife again and approached the blue lit space. Now, without the crumbling walls and creeping moss, the profound eeriness sent a chill down her spine. She could hear the wailing souls, clamoring to escape or be released. Gailin lifted her arm and for once was able to act. She sliced through the membrane and watched with fascination as a soul escaped into the gray world. Nothing blocked her. Drake did not wake her with a strangling grip.

So she sliced again, releasing another and another. The membrane continued to reseal, but she persisted cutting and slashing for what seemed like hours. She could still feel her body jouncing around on the tortured land, but concentrated instead on finishing the job she always intended and if that killed Drake, so be it. He wasn't awake enough to protest and she was sworn to try. Finally, when her knife moved through the thickness and nothing emerged, she stepped back in wonder. Had she finished the job?

With no souls left to release, Gailin removed herself from the gray wasteland of his mind and returned to the real world of rumbling earthquakes to look at the alarming tremblers and saw a huge gash in the earth had widened near them. Hurriedly she took Drake by the arm and dragged him closer to the forest and out of immediate danger of falling into a chasm.

Why save him, she asked herself as she sat back down beside Drake to wait out the geological storm. He had tortured her, manipulated her and used her as a slave, holding her name captive. She could go in now and with a twist of thought remove his brain stem from his skull and be done with him, but something stopped her. The Heart Stone? What had Vamilion said about it being a judge to block you, if you used magic in the wrong way? She really could not justify killing Drake, at least now, as vulnerable as he was, but that didn't mean she couldn't act. Her exploration of the mind made her intimately aware of his hidden secrets.

Reluctantly, she dived back into Drake's mind again and sought out a sealed chamber that held her name. She imagined he had locks and traps on this treasure. Also he would not keep it in a visible place, even if the whole landscape had changed. The gray wasted plain that was his metaphorical mind spread like the sea before her. With a magical sweep of her hand, she brushed the ash away and exposed the cracked and cratered bedrock. Without the foot deep ash to hide under, the scarring of his past showed up as crumbled and tortured slate. And on the slabs of stone she saw a lidded box made of the same cold and brittle rock. She walked to it and then knelt to lift the lid. Inside she found a book exactly like the real one Vamilion had given her.

Without hesitation Gailin lifted the book and inside found all Drake's secrets written inside. His map of the ley lines with the markings visible for her to see, filled one page. On another she found a list of all the things he had learned about the Wise One's magic and even a few things about Vamilion himself that Gailin had not known. On the various pages, like a daily journal, Drake had written the names and sensations he had felt at the death of every soul he had swallowed. Thousands of lives he had taken. It nauseated her as she read his fascination with the ecstasy of a soul leaving a body. It held nothing but pleasure for him, more than he ever felt with Gailin. In that list she found Jonis' name and she mourned for her friend a bit. At least she had been able to free her old beau. Then she returned to the book and saw, on every page written since he had met her, Drake had inscribed her name and beside that word was another name. His.

Neeorm, she read and realized she now had the ability to do to him what he had done to her. Did she have the right? Whatever she did, she decided she would not do it here in the wasteland of his mind. Instead she held the book in her hands and with a wave made the pages blank, like they had never been written. She then put the book back in the box and sealed it beyond ever opening, with wax from her Talisman candle. If Drake even remembered he had a name, he would have to break past her to get to it and then find nothing. And he was far safer without it.

She left Drake's mind and watched from a distance as even the wasteland faded and his mind became a blank slate, empty of every thought he ever held. Even a baby had memories and experiences; cold, warm, sound, sight and pressure from when they were newborn. Gailin had taken him beyond that. Drake might not even have instincts left, and that was fitting in her mind. And the Heart Stone did not block her or give her hesitation for her actions. She had exacted her justice without harming him or others.

Outside the magic realm of Drake's mind, the earth had not settled yet, but the great gashes of tearing and lifting were returning to their former places. Fallen trees did not right themselves but the chasms moved back together and formed a slight scar where the soil had been disturbed. The trees around her stopped dancing and she felt safe enough to stand. From her feet she looked out over the plains and saw a storm in the northwest, but little other activity. She wondered how the village had fared in this epic earthquake. If this destruction had reached from the valley where her palace rose, all the way across the continent to the Don River, the earth must have shifted on its axis and she could well imagine weather would change, seasons perhaps, and people would be frightened. How far reaching was this earthquake?

Vamilion? Was this his work? Suddenly she remembered that she could she reach him now. She had broken Drake's mandate to not perform magic to contact the others, so it stood to reason that she now could do any magic she wished. Gailin immediately sat down beside Drake and pulled out the book Vamilion had given her, intending to write something to see if he would respond. Maybe he was still working his magic and wouldn't reply instantly, but she wanted to write something directly to him, tell him that she was free of Drake's influence and that she had taken the sorcerer as near to death as magic allowed.

She began with Vamilion's name, deliberately addressing her letter to him and smiled as the stylus did not stop or hesitate, but as she went on to continue her thought, something else struck. She stopped and knew she was being called to come to someone's rescue. She didn't hear any words, but the compulsion felt deep and strong. She reached for her candle to travel and hesitated briefly. She couldn't go and leave Drake in a coma on the open plain. She put away the book, reached for Drake's flaccid hand and then used the candle to move inexorably toward where the compulsion guided her.

She arrived, blinded by a lavender light, but it normalized quickly to let her see that she had come somewhere still on the open plains. The stormy weather overhead loomed but as she looked around, Gailin literally saw nothing to use as a landmark except for a trampled and singed ring of grass. And in the middle of the flattened grass lay a man, unconscious and almost crushed as much as the grass. She left Drake where he had arrived beside her and went to this patient, reaching for his mind first to read where his most dangerous injuries might be.

And she met a wall more powerful than any Drake had built. Rather than fight – and fail – to climb over this wall, Gailin did not use magic but instead let his body do the speaking. She could observe the damage with just her hands and eyes. Instinctively she drew her hands down over his long, muscular frame, hovering over tremendous bruises and could feel the profound exhaustion there. Then, when she reached the eighth vertebrae she gasped. About where his ribs stopped, this man's back was shattered. Internal organs were scrambled, but he wouldn't feel the bleeding pressure because there was no way he could feel from the middle of his back on down. Resolutely Gailin continued down the man's body, noting his pelvis and both thigh bones were broken as well. The crushed back probably was a blessing, or the pain would be killing him.

Gailin followed her instincts and imagined there was some way she could knit the nerves and bones together. Unfortunately, this man's personal shields blocked her and she would have to overcome that first if she were to attempt to heal him. She had never dealt with so much internal damage. A burn or a fever, those were things she could see or treat with a medicinal tea. This, pure crushing, would take magic and that meant getting beyond his shield over both mind and body. Gailin tried speaking to him, begging to be invited in. The wounded man retained just enough consciousness to resist, but not enough to accept her help.

Stymied, Gailin sat back in the grass and truly looked at the stranger. He was huge, both tall and strongly built, like he carried great weights for a living. When she picked up his hand, his long roughened fingers spoke of hard work and a powerful stroke if he carried a weapon. She looked, but saw no tools or baggage to indicate his state in life. He was dressed as a worker with sturdy boots and a shirt in need of a wash, unless ash was its original color. He had been outside, even in this winter, for his wind burned face looked summer tan. Very privately she thought of how handsome her patient looked. He had dark hair with a slight wave to it and deep set eyes. On the pretext of trying to see if there was any life to him, she lifted his eyelid and found his stone gray eye staring back at her.

"Sir, you have got to let me help you," she whispered. "You're very badly hurt, but you are shielding me out." The patient didn't acknowledge her, not even with a groan, though his breathing picked up, painful and shallow, gasping like a drowning man. Gailin pulled back her hands and wished there was something she could do.

Then someone spoke, gruff and almost angry behind her, startling her. "Gilead let the Queen do her work. Drop your shields."

Gailin recognized that voice and she bolted to her feet. "Owailion," she whispered, looking down, as if afraid to make eye contact, as he might strike her down, being a full blown King and the first Wise One.

"Go on girl," Owailion ordered impatiently, motioning her to heal the stranger. "He won't fight you anymore."

Obediently Gailin dropped down beside the tall man, Gilead, again. She looked into his mind and found the wall had indeed come down, as if it weren't even there and the image of the man, healthy and whole stood before her. He looked amazing in her mind's eye and she had a hard time concentrating on why she had entered his mind in the first place. "Sir," she told him frankly. "You've been sorely wounded and if I heal you directly, the pain alone may kill you. Therefore I must put you into a deeper sleep. I am only going to let you rest so that you will not be uncomfortable. Please do not fight me."

Gilead's image nodded and Gailin reached into his mind for the one spot that would induce a deep, dreamless release from pain. He slipped away as if night had come into his mind and only the stars – breathing and heartbeat – remained to even indicate he was not as empty as Drake.

Gailin pulled back out of Gilead's now prepared mind and then grounded her own soul before she once again imagined in her mind's eye how that break in his spine actually had happened. It was obvious he had fallen from a great height and several of his damaged ribs had ripped into his liver and spleen. Carefully she used magic movement to nudge the bones out of the organs and sealed them back into place, like the earthquake's terrible chasms had returned to themselves. She saw the free blood pooling in his gut and wondered how to deal with it. Could she just put it back into the circulatory system, moving it from one place to another? She tried this, pouring all the free pooling blood back into the major arteries but this only proved she needed to patch them first, for the fluid all leaked out again before she could address that problem.

How had he survived without any blood remaining in his circulatory system? His heart soldiered on, beating slowly, but moved almost nothing through his system. It seemed miraculous. But rather than having answers for these questions Gailin patiently continued to look for punctures and splits in the blood flow and sealed them in her mind's eye. Then she performed her blood replacement again. She found one additional slit in a vein she had missed and sealed that up as well. She slowly continued with the easier healing: broken hips and leg bones, bruised muscles and impact lacerations before she finally admitted she needed to heal his back.

Gailin felt ready to deal with the spinal injury, having repaired all that was going to pain him once she managed to reestablish feeling in his lower body. She knew sudden shock could kill him just as quickly as a spine injury like this, so she insisted on the induced sleep as well as most of the repair performed first. Clinically Gailin examined the severed spinal column. The broken vertebra had almost been crushed into gravel and it disturbed her. Could she replace it? Should she rebuild it? The torn nerves looked like the frayed rope around her neck at the hanging, ripped and stretched, not cut cleanly. Each nerve would have to mend back to the same exact thread it had been severed from or Gilead's mind would command him to walk and instead he would find himself doing something completely different. And there were thirty-one pairs, left side and right side, of these nerve bundles.

She sat hunched over Gilead's body and began her work, testing each nerve. Her mind reached for the upper strand above the break and felt for its purpose;

lumbar, and then began testing each on the lower half of the break. When she found its match she melded it together, all the way to the molecular level, though she had no idea how she was establishing this. Then she reached for another strand. The effort was exhausting and it took time to find and even more to be sure every single connection was perfect. It would be a shame if Gilead suffered pain or a limp from her work, if he were able to even walk again, just because this was new to her.

And as she worked, Gailin could feel the presence of Owailion hovering beyond her closed mind. He didn't want to interrupt but twice he did, suggesting she stop to eat or rest, but she ignored him as her answer. This was the first time she had done such precision work and Gilead could not afford for her to learn through mistakes. That Owailion remained with her was gratifying, but he really didn't need to do so. She could fend for herself, and yet Owailion stayed on the plains with her, watching to see that nothing else disturbed her and once, as the sun set she felt him place a blanket over her shoulders where she crouched over Gilead's inert body.

Finally, near midnight she had reattached every nerve in the patient's spine and removed the crushed bone. She elected not to try to repair the old vertebra but instead craft a new one out of magic-made bone, wrapping it protectively around his welded spinal column and then replaced the padding between the bones and the cartilage that allowed free movement.

With that she left Gilead's body and opened her non-magical eyes.

The exhaustion descended on her like a bucket of water squashing out a fire. She reeled where she sat and would have fallen had she not already been on the ground. Across from her on the other side of the still unconscious Gilead sat Owailion with his back to a campfire watching her. He huddled under a blanket too, as if the night chill disturbed him but he slowly stretched up and moved stiffly. "Are you ready to eat something now?" he asked simply, his gruff voice chastising her for not taking care of herself. Really she felt little interest in eating but would rather fall asleep right there.

"No, you've got to eat. You're too tired to even know how hungry you should be," Owailion insisted and handed her a bowl of some simple soup. The broth should have smelled wonderful, but it almost revolted her. She vaguely recognized this as a medical condition she should address, but didn't have the wherewithal to actually think about it.

"Eat anyway. It will taste better once you start eating," Owailion replied to her unexpressed thoughts. She had grown too tired to even keep her shields up around him. Owailion's dark eyes flickered over to the patient before he added. "He can wake up in the morning and then you can test your handiwork." So Owailion knew she didn't have the energy to maintain an actual conversation. "I've never seen that kind of magic and it was interesting to watch. I do much of my work in the same manner; looking within something, moving and manipulating it without actually seeing or touching it, but I work on machines, with metal, wood, and other things. You did the same thing but with living tissue. I like watching someone else do it. Very impressive."

Owailion had been right about eating. The moment Gailin managed to get the first spoonful to her mouth she immediately felt hungry and couldn't get it down fast enough. She ate greedily but knew now that she had better ease into it, like a man frozen half to death. You didn't plunge him in the fire to thaw him out. Once finished she set the bowl aside and looked down at her patient. She still didn't have the energy to confront Owailion about what had actually happened here.

"Later. The morning will come soon enough. I will look after him," Owailion assured her. And then suddenly sleep dropped down on Gailin. Her last conscious thought was that Owailion too knew the place in her brain to send her into dreamless sleep.

Chapter 15

Checkmate

Gailin didn't wake at dawn as was her habit, for exhaustion wouldn't allow it, but eventually her own concerns must have driven her awake and she brushed a heavy blanket off her shoulders and sat up on the bare featureless plains. She saw Owailion cooking something over the fire and her patient Gilead remained in the protective sleep she had induced. She looked around and found nothing of Drake. In a panic she stood up, alarmed that he might have regained the ability to leave. She would have bet her Heart Stone that the snake would never walk again, that he had been rendered harmless.

Owailion looked at her with a quizzical eye. "Good morning," he commented. "He's still asleep and you're rested now. Eat and then we can have this discussion."

"Where is the other…" she couldn't say man, for she still doubted Drake's humanity, but she also didn't want to use his name to speak of him, nor show her alarm by questioning his whereabouts.

"I sent him to your old cabin. There's a bed there and he can lie there just as well as here and that way I won't be tempted to murder him anymore. I didn't think you would mind." Owailion passed over a plate of toast and eggs and then turned to begin cooking for himself.

"You know about Drake," Gailin commented between bites. "He...." She really could not speak about what had occurred to her husband. "What happened to him to go into that coma?"

Owailion peered out over the tortured land, now with little sign of the chaos it had endured the day before. "If I'm not mistaken, Vamilion drained the ley lines and without magic the sorcerer could not survive as...as whatever he was."

Gailin shuddered with disgust before she asked, "What was he?"

Owailion snorted with derision. "One step above a snake and several below a man. Like you called him; a Soul Eater. I hope you don't mind me getting rid of him."

"Mind?" Gailin scoffed. "No, I wiped his memory and every bit of knowledge he ever gained but I didn't kill him. I couldn't, I think the Heart Stone blocked me."

"It wouldn't block me," the King of Creating replied frankly. "I just thought I'd better get your input before I did anything more permanent to him. I'm

Owailion by the way. We haven't been formally introduced."

Gailin nodded, but didn't say anything more, seeing as she didn't think using her real name bore
consideration and she had not thought of what to
call herself otherwise. Instead she continued with
the list of questions her mind had gleaned since the
earthquakes began and she had gained the upper
hand over her enemy. "What happened to Drake?
One minute he was ready to use name magic on me
and the next he was practically catatonic. His eyes
just rolled up in his head right after the earthquakes
started. Are the two related?"

Owailion sighed, ignoring his breakfast that began cooling on his plate as he played with his fork,
twisting it into a complicated knot of metal with his
magic. "As I said, it has something to do with the ley
lines. Vamilion and his earthquakes, they cracked the
world open and those such as your Drake, they cannot last without magic in their veins, the magic of
souls or pure magic from the earth. It was one thing
to not be near them. It was a completely different
thing to have them disappear altogether. He needed
the ley lines and they are gone, at least here in the
Land. I hope you weren't too alarmed by what the
Mountain King did."

"No." Gailin shook her head with chagrin. "No, I
just didn't think Vamilion took me seriously when I
spoke about ley lines and the map. He never got back
to me about that. Neither of you wrote back to me
after that so I ended up having to marry Drake."

Owailion straightened out his fork into a thin whip of metal and looked like he might flagellate himself with it before he replied. "That was my fault. I had to egg Vamilion into it. I had to make him so angry that he would break the world and you were the only way. You see, he's the most patient person I've ever met. He has such patience that it is almost impossible to rile him. Simply warning him of attacking waves of sorcerers wasn't enough. He needed to be furious in order to have the momentum to crack the ley lines. Vamilion had to lose you to the Soul Eater in order to build up that pressure, and then I had to pick a fight with him to ignite his anger. He probably still hasn't forgiven me."

The way Owailion carefully flicked his eyes toward her and then her patient, it confirmed her suspicions. "This is Vamilion then, isn't it?" she murmured, unsure if she should feel upset or excited that she was finally meeting her mentor. She should be angry for this epic argument Owailion had apparently devised, forcing her into being with Drake just to enrage Vamilion enough to get the reaction he wanted. She also suspected the King of Creating had probably been responsible or even caused Vamilion's broken back. She indeed felt like a pawn in Owailion's dealings and it seemed that Vamilion was as well. And Owailion still seemed to be manipulating things thinking it was time to force the two to meet face to face. Well, she wasn't going to be a pawn any more. She refused to confront the situation that now had emerged. Vamilion wasn't going to wake up just yet.

Owailion really had no idea the motivations that lurked in the newest Wise One. He continued on, telling her his plan without realizing he wasn't gaining a friend with his forthrightness. "Yes. He called for you just as he ended the destruction, so he must know he needs you finally."

Gailin kept her shields up. "Needs me?" She could not fathom what Vamilion needed from her other than healing. He had been content with Paget. He had been afraid of hurting Gailin and her being manipulated by magic. Vamilion had kept his distance for very good reasons; ones that she agreed with wholeheartedly. She also was not going to let the King of Creating know she would side with Vamilion in almost every instance if it avoided the violence this battle caused.

Owailion let out a disgusted snort, unaware of her distrust in him. "He still hasn't told you, has he? Vamilion needs you and that's why he was so upset when the Soul Eater started using name magic on you. He doesn't want to admit it. Has Vamilion told you that on the day you meet you will be drawn toward each other like a magnet to iron? Has he told you how he felt when you went with the snake off onto the plains? He never did because he has to be forced to see reality."

Gailin tapped deeply into her clinical, emotionless mind before she spoke, lest she slap Owailion. "He told me of the compulsion. Vamilion didn't want my decisions to be pushed on me by magic," she replied slowly, "But he couldn't help my being forced, could he? You were there forcing both of us, instead? You were supposed to take care of me while he took care of my grandmother and instead you abandoned me. And look where we ended up?"

Gailin could hear how her voice was growing more and more bitter, and abruptly she felt no need to stop or control herself. Her anger and frustration that she kept behind her healer's surface now came pouring out at Owailion. "I was forced into a loveless marriage to a man...a snake who basically raped me every day for months. You pressured Vamilion into fighting you, cracking the world open like an egg and broke his back, nearly killing him in the process. Now you are still manipulating us so that we are about to come face to face , even if we don't want to. I won't have it."

Without giving Owailion any warning, Gailin drew the candle from her pack and disappeared. She escaped before Vamilion could wake from her spell. She refused to confront the awkward attraction that had already built up between them. She might want Vamilion with all her soul but she would not force the man she might love into breaking his own vows. And so Owailion was left with nothing but a steel lily that he had formed from his fork and to wait on the plains for the fruits of his plan.

* * *

Vamilion woke slowly. The sun felt luxurious on his face and burned away at the ache that lined his entire body like hoarfrost. He could not remember falling asleep or what had brought him out onto the plains. He wouldn't have come here voluntarily, but he knew where he was in relationship to the mountains before he ever bothered opening his eyes. Even breathing seemed an energy draining effort. Had he been in a battle? Slowly he remembered fighting Owailion but he could not recall why. It had something to do with a lightning storm and earthquakes. A volcano?

Someone nearby moved, pacing back and forth and Vamilion could hear the grass brush against someone's legs. Did he have the energy to open his eyes to see? When Vamilion stretched out his magical mind, it hurt to try, but he came up against an alarmingly familiar wall; Owailion. Had his adversary come to finish the task of killing him? Why was Owailion hovering if the battle was finished? They couldn't actually kill each other – unless this was being dead. Well, Owailion could kill him with his name but if that was the goal, he hadn't done it in the past twenty-five years.

"I know you're awake in there," Owailion grumbled. "Are you hungry?"

That didn't sound like someone willing to strike him down with a lightning bolt again. Besides, the warmth of the sun told him the sky was clear; no lightning ready to strike. Reluctantly Vamilion opened his eyes. "It hurts to lift my eyelids," he replied in a cracking voice. Crack? That word running through his head brought other memories. He had cracked the earth. What had he done? His fingers ached from the effort of crushing stone and his back bowed in memory of lifting whole mountains of earth. He might be a big, strong body but no one should lift mountains. It hurt too much.

"The Queen healed your back." Owailion then put a full plate on Vamilion's chest just to expedite his waking. "You should probably thank her by doing something towards your survival."

That comment got Vamilion's eyes to open up more fully and a flood of memories came rushing in. Gailin, the pain, calling her, he had poured the ley lines out of existence. Had he really broken his back? No, Owailion had done that for him but apparently he held no grudge seeing as the King of Creating was making him breakfast. At last, with the blue sky overhead and memories back in place Vamilion decided he could not sleep forever. Carefully he lifted the breakfast plate away and sat up. That he could do so was a miracle.

"She's good," Owailion commented from the safety of the far side of a campfire. "But she also left before you woke up."

Vamilion chuckled painfully. "Good for her," he commented and began eating slowly. "She knows why I don't want to meet face to face and respects it....unlike you."

"Are you trying to pick a fight with me again?" Owailion muttered in disgust. "She's your mate and we will need her before year's end. There is another attack, remember? That ship you intercepted was a feint. The main body is coming from the south west, a combination of Marewn and Demonian sorcerers. We cannot hope to block them all."

Vamilion sighed with exhaustion despite the rest he had recently acquired. "The Queen will help if we ask her to come, and she doesn't have to meet me to do that," he replied and then stopped as he speculated on something. "Is that why you allowed her to go off with the snake and then get pregnant by him as well? You wanted to breed more magicians? That's beneath even your harsh methods."

Owailion rolled his eyes in disgust. "I've told you before. Wise Ones can't pass on their magic to another. We cannot have children, and no, I wouldn't have done that. I had other reasons for getting you down off your mountain top."

Vamilion clenched his teeth in anger, refusing to let go of the one implied comment. "Wait, you are saying the Queen cannot have children, but...."

"And you can't either. Your boys aren't your boys. No Wise One can reproduce." Owailion said the strange sentences slowly, bitterly, and it sounded like he had actually practiced this conversation so he would finally make himself clear.

Vamilion carefully set down the plate he had slowly been eating from, appalled by this revelation from Owailion. He was glad Gailin wasn't here for this either, for he was fairly sure he was going to punch the King of Creating in the face if he could scrounge up the energy to stand. How could Owailion say that about his sons? He implied that Paget....

"She wasn't faithful to you Gilead," Owailion reiterated. "You've been putting your devotion into a relationship, an oath that she broke years ago, before you were ever a Wise One. You just assumed that your children were yours and that you didn't have any more children because you became a magician later. In fact, you've always been a magician and those boys aren't yours. If you don't believe me..."

Vamilion finally struggled to his feet with effort. It took a moment for him to gain his balance and then he looked down at Owailion from his considerable height with an amazing mix of emotions: roiling anger, disgust, a profound grief, amazement and wonder. Part of him wanted to begin a physical brawl. He would have been able to kill Owailion in a fist fight or swords if they had both been simply men. He probably had half a foot and fifty pounds on his peer, but that was not where their battles would take them. In emotional battles, Owailion had far more practice and ammunition. He knew how to drive in that knife. And truth drove every word. A Wise One could not lie.

"Go and ask her," Owailion whispered, still sitting beside his fire, no longer caring to see the agony he had caused in the Mountain King's eyes.

Vamilion looked out over the plains as if he wanted nothing better than to do just that, but there wasn't a single mountain in view and not even the dark line of forest or river to give him some sense of where he had landed. He would only weaken his already unsteady recovery if he tried to leave this spot. And Vamilion didn't want to go speak with Paget. Indeed, he preferred to seek for years for a way to not have to confront what she had done. Why would his wife be unfaithful to him? True, he had been a trader and away from their home often during the early part of their marriage, but she had never expressed discontent with that way of life. Vamilion had tried to be a considerate husband and when they were together they had enjoyed each other passionately. Why would she deceive him? And why had he not known all these years?

"You never went into Paget's thoughts without permission," Owailion supplied, still not looking away from the fire. "Your honor made you vulnerable to her deception, even before you touched the Heart Stone."

Defeated and beyond words, Vamilion sat down again with a thump. "Why are you telling me this now, here, where .... where I cannot escape your toxic words?"

Owailion tugged a tuft of grass from the ground and fed it to the fire, although it didn't need to burn anything more than his magic. "I have always wanted you to go to your true mate. You know that. I want that because you will both be stronger for it."

"What's it to you?" Vamilion muttered bitterly. "You and magic have ruined every grain of happiness I ever had."

Owailion plucked up a shapeless glob of metal he had dropped earlier in the grass and began playing with it like it was clay, shaping wondrous little miniature dragons and monsters every time he closed his hand over the mass. His mindless creating might be to distract Vamilion, but it failed. Owailion's answer was far more important. "I did it because your grain of anger will dislodge a pebble, which will nudge a rock that will launch an avalanche of magic that will block evil from invading for another five hundred years. Because you are the only person in the world I can call my friend. Because you deserve to be happy if anyone does."

Happy? The word seemed beyond recognition. Vamilion didn't feel capable of happiness. He would rather battle a thousand invading sorcerers than to talk to Paget or Gailin at that moment. He might start walking and see where he ended up before he had a single word to give to either woman.

Instead he spoke again to stop his mind from fixating. "So you made me angry enough to snap the ley lines," he managed to say, finally recognizing Owailion's motives for letting Gailin be manipulated by the hunter. "Is there any way you can make me sad enough to bury every sorcerer in the world?"

"No," Owailion admitted regretfully. "But I can make you happy enough to fight them."

Vamilion sighed. The King of Creating still wanted him to go look Gailin in the eye and forget about Paget forever. "No," he finally decided. "I will have to confront Paget first. And you will have to send me there if you want it to happen in the next two months, because it will take me that long to walk off this plain. Send me to a mountain and I'll do it."

Chapter 16

Confrontation

Gailin found Drake in the bed she had abandoned months ago, lying deathly pale. She could not imagine how she could deal with the remains of her husband and still go on Seeking like she felt compelled to do. She wanted to move on, finding other Talismans, helping people all across the Land. The recent destruction must have caused a myriad of injuries that would need her help, but she didn't know how to uphold both her responsibilities as a Wise One and a wife. Technically, Drake was still alive and she had an obligation to him. What could she do?

She looked around the empty cabin and only then realized that Grandma's bed was gone, along with its former occupant. Where had Vamilion taken her grandmother? Where would she be? He would have found some way to take care of her, even if he was battling Owailion and all the sorcerers in the world. He kept his promises, of that she was sure. Where would he have taken her grandmother? Gailin deliberately took out her book and wrote an urgent question to Vamilion. She didn't want to interrupt him intentionally, and she doubted his dealings with Owailion had resolved themselves so quickly, but she needed to know her grandmother was safe and find someplace for Drake.

An idea occurred to her even as she wrote her question and then closed the book. Could she find her grandmother herself? She sat at her abandoned table to think it out and concentrate. She had been given the candle that provided instant travel but no way to find where she wanted to go. She had been drawn to the unknown location in the middle of the plains because Vamilion had called her. Could she use that same method to find her grandmother? Grandma's name, she knew. She could go to Grandma with the candle if she knew where to find her. Carefully, Gailin concentrated and conjured herself a map.

Vamilion's map of the world, overlain with Drake's ley lines appeared on the table before her. She did not remember it herself precisely, but the map she had found in her husband's memory had become part of the magic in her mind and created itself flawlessly on the paper that spread before her. She recognized pieces of it from her limited travel and was able to label some things from what she knew of maps in general. This one, however, had few markings for actual human habitation and no words at all. It had originally been a geological map and then Drake had marked the ley lines and Wise One palaces over the top so she would have to use what she already knew.

She found where her home village must lay, on the Don River, halfway between the Vamilion Mountains and the southern end of the Great Chain. Drake and she had walked northwest onto the plains and she traced that direction from her village with her finger. Somewhere to the northwest on a second river and near the mountains she had married Drake in the town of Meeting, which was not noted on the map. Then they had passed into the mountains going to the base of a huge lake where they found the Apothecary. Then they wove their way west until they came to her palace in the mountains. It was marked with a diamond shape, one like fifteen others all around the map. A smile came to her face as she set her finger there. One day she would return, make the shattered, avalanche-blasted cabin disappear and return to open the doors of that palace, but not today. If she were in the Great Chain then the other line of mountains in the south must be the Vamilion Mountains. He had been named after that range... or it could be the other way around. However, only one Wise One palace had been built in those mountains and that would be Vamilion's home.

He would have taken Grandma there, she was sure. Gailin rose from the table and stepped outside as if she could see directly there. The day was still young and would be even younger there. Could she go to a place she had not seen or was not called? Experimenting for the first time with her limits, Gailin reached her mind toward the west to seek her grand-mother's dreams. The old woman's thoughts would be quiet and peaceful, tired and unclear. At first Gailin struggled with focusing her mind's eye, getting tangled in the minds of others along the way. There were many villages along the western branch of the Don and every one of them had emergencies and urgent healing needed due to the geologic upheaval of the day before. She would have to come back this way and knew that compulsions to go help lined up as she traveled down the river and along the mountains. But she must settle Drake first.

Finally, in the mind's eye of one traveler she encountered she saw Vamilion's palace at last. He wasn't even aware of her invasion as he hiked down a lonely road into a town at the base of the mountains. The graceful edifice she saw through his vision had been cut into the mountain itself, white and stunning, with spires and intricate pointed arches as a recurring theme in its architecture. The black slate roofs topped with blood red banners towered over the trees and village below. The iron gates and intricate gardens fascinated her. Cinder pathways through the gardens crunched under the traveler's feet. Like her, this wanderer also could not take his eyes off the glittering walls. He too felt her awe of Vamilion, home of the Mountain King.

Gailin pulled her mind back into her humble cabin and considered what she would do now. She had a visual to use if she traveled by candle, but dare she go to Vamilion's palace? Paget was there watching over

Grandma. Would she know Gailin for who and what she was? Would Vamilion's wife be willing to take another invalid? Well, it didn't matter. Gailin had too much to do and taking Drake with her would not be possible any more than leaving him here to starve in an empty cabin. She had to do it and face the consequences later.

"Neeorm," Gailin said with authority, wondering if he had the capability to follow instructions with his empty mind. "Wake up."

Drake's eyes opened, though they appeared cloudy and he didn't turn to look at her. "Neeorm, sit up," she commanded.

In an eerie move, the almost-dead sat up in the bed where Owailion had dropped him. Gailin smiled at what she could do to him now, and while she thought of torturing the sorcerer for what he had done to her, she didn't have time and the Heart Stone had other dealings with her. Drake still wore only his night clothes so she conjured boots and britches onto him before ordering him out of bed and to follow her outside. A wicked part of her hoped he recognized how name magic manipulated him but it didn't matter now. She took him by the arm, lifted her candle high and concentrated on the path to Vamilion's palace. Then she stepped toward where the light led her.

The sun was higher here, barely noon, and Gailin began walking down the cinder path, seeing the spires and sheer walls through the trees for herself. However, Drake didn't follow her walking and instead fell on his face before she remembered she would need to give him every instruction. "Neeorm, stand up and follow me," she commanded. The humiliation would be horrible for a man like Drake, but she wouldn't torment him any more than this. She walked him through glorious gardens and past ponds and the park-like setting. It was a pleasant place that he wouldn't be able to appreciate and that was good enough.

When Gailin faced the polished wood door, shining with redwood stain to a high gloss, she knew now how difficult this was going to be for her as well. Gailin took a steadying breath. She was about to meet Paget, the woman she would eventually supplant in Vamilion's heart. Gailin did not want this to be a confrontation but it was doomed to be awkward at the least if Paget knew who she was. And who was she? She could never use the name Gailin again. She had to use another name. And the instant she thought of this, she knew the name she would use; her grandmother's. It was fitting. She reached out and knocked as loudly as she could.

The door, all two stories of it opened after only a moment and much to her surprise a man answered the door. "Good afternoon," he said politely. "How may I help you?"

"I've come to see my grandmother. I'm..." Abruptly she found herself blocked. She couldn't even lie about her name? For one flustered moment Gailin almost panicked. Then she recalled how Vamilion had introduced himself to her. "You may call me Honiea. I am the Queen of Healing."

The gentleman who opened the door looked at her with suddenly wide eyes and then bowed low to her, opened both doors and motioned for her to come in. "I am Goren, the Doorkeeper of Vamilion. You are most welcome," he intoned, almost reverently.

Gailin had to order Neeorm through the doors into a wondrous foyer lined with velvet hangings over sheer marble walls. She gazed in fascination at crystal chandeliers and polished onyx floors. She had never imagined such a place. Her eyes were drawn to all the little niches around the walls. Each one housed a delicate sculpture of some animal or plant exquisitely crafted out of marble or some other stone. She looked at them in awe, just then realizing that Vamilion must have been their creator. He had a gift with stone, he had said and now she saw it in action. When he wasn't off fighting to save the world and cracking the earth in two, he came home for peace and worked with his hands. It was charming to her and she felt the tug of a compulsion. She could easily fall in love with this sculptor.

Goren smiled at her distraction and Gailin felt herself blushing in front of him. "I'm sorry. They're beautiful...the whole place is beautiful...but I didn't come here to...I came to see my grandmother and...and this is Neeorm. He is....broken. I need a place to put him. He cannot....I need your help with him. Is that possible?"

Goren looked severely at Drake and the door steward's visage darkened. "He is the hunter that has plagued Lord Vamilion for many years. You have mastered him then?"

"I have. He deserves death, but magic has stayed my hand. His true name is Neeorm. After all the earthquakes yesterday, there is much I must go do and I cannot watch over him and still do my duty. He is catatonic and will probably die soon, but until that time, he must be cared for. Is that possible here?"

Goren looked doubtful. "I am not a magician to be commanding him. I don't have the power to do name magic but if he is not a danger to others here..."

"He will be well here," a woman's voice echoed down from one of the spiraling stairs above the foyer.

Gailin looked up and saw an older lady with graying black hair running in long braids down her back and deep brown eyes. The lines of time had begun pulling on her but she retained a tall dignity that Gailin could never hope to have. Even in her royal gown and standing in her palace Gailin would never hope to be as grand as Paget in Vamilion's eyes. His wife was tall and graceful, a fine match at one time for the likes of Vamilion. Her coloring, equally dark and dramatic went well with the palace she called home and Gailin felt like the intruder she was. Paget wore a fine silk dress, night blue and devoid of all decoration that all the better showed off her alabaster skin and lonely face.

Without realizing it, Gailin lowered her head to honor Vamilion's wife. "Lady Paget," she murmured. "Thank you...for the care of my grandmother as well. The Land is new and there is no place to house such as these. One day there will be, but until then..."

"Until then, I will watch them," Paget replied as she came down the stairs and stood in front of Gailin, looking her over. The older woman's face was hard to read, almost like Drake's, for her eyes also looked deep and emotion seemed alien to her. Gailin felt tempted to listen in on Paget's thoughts to see if she knew about the compulsion that drew Vamilion and Gailin together, but she resisted. She did not want to know if Paget approved or disapproved of her but it could hardly be comfortable to look at the other woman who would follow after you.

"My thanks. If I could see my grandmother very quickly, I will be gone," Gailin nervously added.

Both Goren and Paget objected. "Surely you can stay for lunch at least," suggested Goren. Perhaps they were unaware of who she really was and all the awkwardness her presence must bring through their doors.

Gailin sighed with regret as well as to ease the tension she felt. "I'm sorry, I cannot. I am the Queen of Healing and there is much that is demanding my attention. It is a compulsion..." Now Paget had to know.

Paget looked down, almost with sadness in her eyes. "I hear that word, compulsion, often. I'm sorry. I will take you to your grandmother."

Gailin followed Paget to a door just off the foyer to where her grandmother had been warmly housed. There was a fire at a brazier with her concoction simmering over it and the room smelled deliciously of the honey in the kettle. Grandmother lay in the same rustic bed that must have come with her from the cabin. It didn't fit the fine decoration of the gold and green room with elegantly cast candlesticks but no one complained. Gailin went to Grandma's side and put her hand on her pale face, listening intently to her grandmother's thoughts and dreams. The old woman slept contentedly and was in no pain. With a bit of concentration Gailin was able to wash away the bed sores that invariably developed with time though there was nothing to prevent them.

"She'll not make it to winter," Paget murmured from the door.

"I know," Gailin replied, not taking her eyes off the woman she loved. "I just wanted to say goodbye. I wasn't able to do so before. I will leave you a candle. Just light it and hold it up high and I will know you need me if... when she is about to pass. Or whenever you need my help. Your husband promised to take care of her and I thank you for what you have done."

"It is the least I could do," Paget replied graciously. "I might not have magic, but I have served it most of my life."

Gailin looked back at Paget at that and then smiled. "Oh, you have magic, Lady. You have love which is the strongest magic in the world. It can... it has moved mountains."

Paget leaned wearily against the door jam, as if she had grown too tired to stand. "That was him yesterday, wasn't it? He was moving mountains. How was it?" she asked, although she obviously knew the answers.

Gailin stood and moved toward the door, for she did not want her grandmother to be tainted by the discussions of magic. "Yes, he was moving more than mountains, but I don't know much about how, or even why. We have not…not formally met. He still cares for you and will not break his vow to you. I respect him for that. There is much for me to learn and do in the meantime and it will be many years before I am…ready. You need not worry that I will ever take your place in his heart."

Gailin then passed hurriedly through the door and left the room, afraid of seeing the pain in the older woman's eyes, passing beyond Paget and back into the foyer. But as she left the room, she heard Paget's parting words. "No, but I have already taken myself out of his heart."

* * *

In the end Vamilion talked Owailion into sending him to the new Gardway island with an oath that he would confront Paget, but he wanted to be clean and rested first and somehow, after a transcontinental battle, a winter as a cairn of stones, cracking the world open and then having his body pieced back together, he wanted a bath. Besides, this conversation required some thought and stranded on the plains, with Owailion hovering over him didn't count as adequate preparation to speak about this. So he had

Owailion send him in one of his instant travel spells to Gardway Island.

Uncharacteristically Owailion placed him gently right beside one of the still steaming pools and it was a good thing. Vamilion could barely stand and while everything functioned, moving still felt incredibly painful and slow, like he had aged decades into an old man. "You are one," he muttered to himself as he stripped down and eased himself carefully into the water. The tsunamis from the season before had left mud deposits over the black lava fields and a green haze of plant life had begun, leaving the alien territory smoothed and almost like a carpet. The hot springs steamed invitingly, but after soaking there in the warm water for an hour and surveying his handiwork now that the volcanic unrest had settled, Vamilion finally realized he would have to think about Paget no matter what he did.

First, Paget had been unfaithful to him. Granted it had been years ago, before he ever touched the Heart Stone, but he could not fathom why she would have done that and it should be the first question he asked of her. It was difficult to decide which emotion he wanted to vent with her first; sadness or anger. In the end he decided last fall's battle had been enough anger for the time being without dealing with his wife's unfaithfulness and wanted to explore something new. Maybe he had been a difficult husband and not noticed the ways he would have failed her. No, he would not have changed much. He had been himself and she could not fault him for that. It might not have been easy to be married to a man who traveled much of the time, but how else would he have made a living back then, before magic?

So how was he going to confront her? The older Paget grew the more gentle he found himself with her. He wanted to give her everything her heart desired and with his magic he had. She lived in luxury in his palace, with fine clothes and jewels he mined and polished himself. She could travel if she desired, but she never expressed that as an ambition. She had a few close friends in the village that had formed around the palace after he had broken the seal to it, and occasionally she would invite them to her home. She gardened passionately and had taken up painting at the same time Vamilion had discovered his love of sculpting, so they could work together. Was their relationship perfect? Certainly not, but he never knew she had anything to be discontented over.

However, there remained the fact that she was going to die and he was still the thirty-three year old he had been on the day he touched the Heart Stone. Her infidelity had been long before that and now Vamilion felt the anger setting in again. It made the water hotter as he thought of it. Paget had allowed him to believe both their sons were his and he had raised them as such, loving them. He would have loved them even had he known, but did the boys realize he wasn't their real father as well now? Would Paget have told them?

Oh, this was getting him nowhere. He would never know until he asked her. He couldn't imagine who she had been with and felt revolted by the thought. His love for Paget had never wavered and wouldn't now, though he wanted to be upset with her. Mostly he wanted a reason why and an opportunity to somehow forgive her.

Then there was the King of Creating to consider. Owailion had essentially thrown Gailin to the wolves, almost encouraging her to marry the Soul Eater and prove that Wise Ones could not have children in order to witness this to Vamilion. Owailion probably had other motives for this epic argument he had crafted, such as making Vamilion angry enough to break the ley lines. But why now? Gailin was so new to magic that it was not right to use her like a pawn to motivate him and that was no way to drive her into power. Was the impending invasion so alarming to him that he wanted Gailin abused and... He couldn't bear to think about that either. Surely there were better ways to prepare for an invasion.

Night descended on the island, leaving Vamilion in the dark, echoing how he felt emotionally. In the morning he would go confront Paget and hope for the best though he did not know how he could look at her the same way ever again. He pulled himself out of the pool and conjured a comfortable mat and blanket. Then he curled up on the edge of the pool and slept deeply, though he had to use magic to put himself at ease and his tortured body wasn't the only thing keeping him awake.

At dawn Vamilion rose, conjured himself a new set of clothes with less lightning singes and was thinking about shaving. Paget never liked him to wear a beard, though it helped him blend in with the miners that worked the mountains around their home and it made him look a little older, like he fit with his wife. He conjured the razor but then thought better of it. Paget's feelings about his appearance were hardly his problem, and he would go as he was. So he ate breakfast sitting on the green moss lining the pool and was just thinking about shifting to the top of the volcano so he could look before he left. Then something changed.

"Lord Vamilion, you must come home immediately." The mind voice of Goren, his Doorkeeper echoed through Vamilion's soul. Goren rarely panicked and with magic limited to calling to his master and a long life, the man was not likely to delve into Vamilion's mind at a whim. He could count on one hand how many times Goren, a stable and almost emotionless man, had called him in the twenty-three years they had known each other.

"I'll be there in a minute," Vamilion shot back just to reassure him and leapt to his feet and then to the mountain palace. He bolted to the polished door and burst through before Goren would have made it down the stair to the door to meet him.

Goren greeted him at the foyer. "My Lord," he whispered in his distress. "I'm so glad you've come. It's the Lady Paget. She's fallen suddenly ill...I think..."

"Goren, where is Paget?" Vamilion demanded, feeling a sudden crushing fear. He had to speak with her. She couldn't die. Vamilion didn't wait for the older gentleman to spit out the words. He knew where Paget would be; in their bedroom near the top of the main tower of the palace. She loved that room and he shifted there without hearing Goren's explanation.

The room was dark. Goren must have come to tend the lights and found her there, remaining in bed long after her normal time to be up and about. But Paget lay in the bed, her eyes closed and breathing shallowly. She had grown pale as the pillow on which she rested. Her dark hair still lay in the braid she normally wore when she went to bed and on the nightstand stood a goblet half full of some strange, thick liquid. Vamilion lifted it to sniff the drink and almost gagged. Poison? He couldn't be sure.

All his former emotion fled as he reached out to touch her pale face where the lines of her age had deepened and a pain wrote itself in her hands. He wished, not for the first time, that his hands were more gentle, not half stone and rough, as he brushed against her cheek. He never made it a habit to go into her mind out of respect for the inherent inequality of their relationship, but not now. Vamilion used his touch to form the conduit to her sleeping mind.

Dark and pained, he sensed the poison she had taken was working its way through her system. However, more grating was her own unrest. Guilt or some other misery had driven her to this point and Vamilion could sense how she wallowed in it. No specifics leapt out at him, but he knew she had done this to herself because of her personal chaos. It burned through her dreams and drove her to end her life without resolving what truly tortured her.

"Paget," he commanded, using name magic on her for the first and only time, "wake up and talk to me, please." He could not bear that she would leave him and not tell him where he had gone wrong. He had always known he loved her and would lose her, but not now, not yet, not with so much unresolved.

Obediently, Paget's deep brown eyes opened and focused on him. She even managed a smile. Exhaustion wrote itself in the dark under her eyes, making them seem more alluring and mysterious. That he was there was a comfort to her and she patted the bed, inviting him to sit rather than kneel. Whatever was in the goblet moved slowly and he had time. Without daring to consider the ramifications he reached out his mind and bespoke the Queen of Healing.

"Gailin, please come to me."

While he waited, he leaned down and kissed Paget good morning and she didn't, for once reject him. She still loved him, he realized, even as she was fleeing from this life, from him.

"Why?" he asked simply.

Paget didn't speak at first and he could feel her tremendous exhaustion. The poison would put her to sleep until she had no energy to breathe or keep her heart beating, but painless and slow nonetheless. Come on, Gailin, hurry please.

"The Queen of Healing came here yesterday," Paget managed to say, looking away. "She's a lovely girl."

"That's not the reason you are leaving me," Vamilion replied, struggling mightily to keep the bitterness out of his voice. "You've been leaving me for years now, and I need to know why. The boys are...."

She knew immediately what he inferred and almost welcomed the opportunity to bare her soul. "I tried so hard not to be lonely when you were away. I wanted you to have children and when I couldn't give them to you...I wanted to give you something. It was wrong, but I wanted the children too. They might not be yours but I would never tell them. I loved you and I'm sorry it hurt you. I did it for love."

The left over stiffness in Vamilion's back shifted into stone and he felt ill, as if he too had swallowed poison. Why was hearing the words admitted so much more painful than being simply told she had been unfaithful? "Who?" Vamilion managed to ask.

The dying woman sighed with regret. "I don't know. Both...as soon as you had left so you would never know or suspect. You would think they were yours. I chose the men because they looked a little like you – dark and stormy." She reached out her hand and with effort touched his face.

He couldn't resist, but gathered her into his arms and held her tight. He had always loved the feel of her head against his chest so that she could hear his heart beating. It had become a reminder that he was still human, despite all the changes he had undergone. A human heart could love. She fell asleep often listening to that steady rhythm over the years. Now he held her, hoping that she would hear that beat and keep her own heart going for a little longer.

Too late, Vamilion magically heard the knock at the door and Goren answering, ushering his future into his house. The doorkeeper hurried the Queen of Healing up the stairs, practically running, but it would be too late. Paget had escaped the awkwardness of her life, leaving him free and in more pain than a broken back had prepared him for. Gailin reached the doorway, and he didn't turn back to look at her. Not yet. He had an oath to keep.

Vamilion might have hoped that Gailin could do something, but it was everlastingly too late. They could both smell the poison and magical ears witnessed the silence of the woman's heart. It didn't take too much to understand what had happened. He could only hope that Gailin's coming the day before had not precipitated this decision. Vamilion's pain, as his wife's faded, rippled like an earthquake through the room and he could only pray that Gailin did not think that she had made it worse.

Goren and Gailin stood watch in the doorway, waiting until Vamilion finally lay Paget back down in the bed. Gently, he arranged her hair and folded Paget's hands gently on the cover. He studied her visage for the longest time, memorizing it for the future. He would sculpt her one day and every crease and vein within her hands would be lovingly reproduced. It was strange that neither the anger, nor the grief over her decisions won out in his heart. Instead it was the love that remained behind.

Chapter 17

Laying the Lines

Gailin wondered privately, behind her strongest shields, if Vamilion would have been more amazing if he wasn't grieving, but something stirred in her soul as she watched him slowly, stiffly stand. Should she leave, letting him settle his fractured world before he took up new pieces and started a new life with the compulsion to love her? She had already seen him, unconscious on the plains, and felt that stirring but it would grow stronger if she let him in now, comforting him.

"Should I go?" she whispered mentally to him, looking at his stooped back and not feeling a single shard of pride at what she had done that this tall, powerful man could walk again.

"No, Goren will take you to the Truth Chamber. I'll be there briefly. I'll....I'll need your help."

Goren must have been included in the private conversation, at least partially. The doorkeeper turned in the passageway and motioned for her to go ahead of him and he would lead the way to this Truth Chamber. Gailin walked numbly through the glorious, richly decorated halls and wondered why she was even there. She had not come in time to save Paget. She did not feel welcome when she had probably been the reason the Lady had taken the poison and out in the Land, people were suffering and she wanted to go help. She had just started her work in the village she had chosen with her candle when Vamilion's call had come, desperate for her help. And she had failed him.

"Thank you for coming," Goren said in a flat, emotionless voice as they walked down a set of stairs. "He will need you at this painful time. It is so sad that...that she did this to herself."

"Were you close to the lady?" Gailin asked, struggling for something to say.

Goren shrugged awkwardly. "As a door steward, it's not in my nature...you might even call it a compulsion, to connect with anyone but Lord Vamilion. It is part of the extremely long life with which I've been blessed. I've never felt any need to do anything but serve. It might seem strange but I'm actually older than he is, but with far less experience. Essentially it is my compulsion to be his friend and therefore, to take care of Lady Paget was part of that, but I wasn't close to her. I cannot imagine life without her about the house, but I'll grieve more for him than for her. Does that sound harsh, when I spent more time with her really than he could?"

Gailin looked at the non-descript, unassuming gentleman and wondered what she could say. "No, it must be a little like being a healer. I have to inflict pain and sometimes give bad news to some people and in order to do that duty, I cannot afford to have emotions that show. It's almost easier to heal people I don't know because the concern for their feelings does not interfere with worry over their grief. In a way it is a gift I must have. Perhaps it is the same for you."

Goren stopped in the hallway, looking at her in wonder. "That is precisely what it is," he commented. "You are truly a Wise One, Lady Honiea."

"I don't feel very wise right now. Was my coming here the reason why she took poison?" she asked.

Goren shook his head and then unexpectedly reached for a door set into the hall across from an exquisite stained glass window of a mountain peak lined with snow. "No, my Lady. That pain was as old as the hills and the thaw is coming. The danger for avalanche is always greatest then and it was bound to happen. If I had known, I would have stopped her, but I suspect she had been dosing herself for several days before you came. She had been ill and there was little any of us could do."

Goren motioned for her to enter the exquisite room beyond the intricately carved door and she stepped in expecting to find much the same beauty witnessed throughout the castle but as she stepped over the threshold, she shifted into her regalia, lavender and silver, but this time without the weapons.

Instead she wore a veil of the thinnest gauze, held down by a crown of silver and diamond. She gasped and turned back toward Goren, looking at him as if he had cast a spell over her.

"The Truth Chamber is enchanted," he explained from the safety of the hallway. "Any who enter are shown as their true self and you, my Lady, are a Queen. I shall bring you something to eat and Lord Vamilion will be up when he is ready. Please, make yourself at home." Then the doorkeeper turned and left her.

Reluctantly Gailin remained in the richly appointed chamber. The walls glistened with quartz and windows cut of the stuff, thin enough to let in the bright sun, but still white with the carvings showing thicker with the familiar outline of the Great Chain Mountain range. The furnishings shone of polished bronze and cut jewels, mostly ruby and onyx on the gray velvet chairs and polished bronze table. Blood red velvet hangings adorned the spaces without windows, and she couldn't resist drawing her hands through the fabric but this exposed that behind each drapery a sculpture stood. A statue of Owailion she recognized. Behind another she found a woman in alabaster hidden away and she knew instinctively that this must be Raimi, Owailion's dead wife. With a quick look she counted sixteen hidden alcoves and she knew then what Vamilion was creating here: the meeting place of the Wise Ones, crafted in anticipation. She dare not look further, afraid she would find Vamilion or herself reproduced in stone.

With trepidation, Gailin sat at the table and tried not to feel uncomfortable in the lavender gown. At least it was fitting for such a grand place. She feared to think what she must look like. Numbness and feeling emotionally overwrought must appear on her face. Somehow honey hair and freckles with green eyes did not fit here. This was not her home, but she knew it fit perfectly as Vamilion's refuge. He stood strong, tall and brooding, like the ceiling overhead with obsidian beams arching over marble walls. She looked at the jewels set in the table top and had to reach out to touch them, ensuring they were real. She touched a diamond frozen in the bronze and then compared it to the ones that lined her veil. The same, she realized with wonder. It was real.

Disturbed, she lifted the veil over her head so she could see more clearly. Could she be 'at home' here as Goren had advised her? No, not until she knew how Vamilion faired. Not until she knew him and he knew her. This room might show her as a Queen here, but she clashed and she still felt as an interloper, needing to be out in the Land, finding her Talismans and healing the people. It felt like a compulsion...an itch Vamilion had called it, but she could resist. If she concentrated, the King of the Mountain's need also fit in that compulsion and she knew she would have to face him and his grief before she could answer the other needs.

Goren returned momentarily with a silver tray of tea, crackers and fruit. As he came in, the doorkeeper did not change a bit, retaining his simple gray suit and solemn appearance, as if he were one of Vamilion's sculptures come to life. Unexpectedly though, he sat down at the table to keep her company and poured tea. They ate in silence at first and waited, like they were a patient's loved ones, expecting a grim diagnosis. Gailin instinctively knew that conversation would be awkward and oppressive at this dark time.

Finally, when the light had begun to fade in the stone windows, Gailin heard the door open again and turned to see Vamilion enter the room. He looked so different from how he had on the plain, crumpled and crushed, gray like stone and in pain. Now she expected much the same thing. She was wrong. The man who entered now transformed. He stood tall, at least a foot taller than her and while his dark hair and gray eyes brooded like a storm over a mountain top, she knew instinctively he would never be cold with her. His hands, strong and roughened with the stone he worked, would not harm her or suck their life from her, but he was independent and gentle with them, despite their size. And when he stepped into the room, he became a king. The striking burgundy tunic in leather, studded with gems in the outline of mountains brought out his wind tanned skin and the patent leather baldric carried a chisel, hammer, pick and even a sword, all finely polished. Vamilion, well accustomed to the shifting he made when coming into this room, lifted the baldric over his head and set it by the door, looked over at her. Gailin stood up to meet him.

And she had the thrill of seeing Vamilion's eyes widen in wonder. He stopped, frozen in the door frame in wonder. She felt much the same way. She felt lightness that defied explanation given the grim circumstances of this first official meeting. She experienced a comfort and attraction completely missing from her tense relationship with Drake or her disinterest with Jonis. Vamilion fit comfortably in her mind, as if they could be in a room together forever, with no need to interact, and it would not feel awkward in the least. Yet she wanted to be with him.

She managed to speak first. "If this is not the right time... I will go and..."

"No," he interrupted and managed to take a step. "I need you to be here." The pleading in his voice belied his reluctance to approach her. Why she needed to remain when he needed to grieve disturbed her, but when he finally took a few more steps and came to the table to sit, she joined him at the table and served him the tea that she magically warmed for him. Somehow Goren had taken himself away without either of them noticing, knowing this conversation needed to be private.

Gailin instinctively recognized Vamilion needed to do the speaking, slowly unraveling his thoughts and emotions, for he had buried them like jewels in a mine and had never dug them free until now. He had to find them or he would never be able to truly overcome all that he had experienced. Slowly, he evolved into the man to whom she would bind herself.

"Thank you," he began slowly in his deep voice, gentle and yet gravelly. "You rebuilt my body and I didn't get to tell you how much I appreciate your healing."

"Does everything work right?" she asked and then realized how awkward that sentence might be taken. She blushed and wished that the veil was back over her face. Vamilion didn't chuckle, taking her comment as nothing more than her medical curiosity.

"It's fine. I'm stiff and sore, but then...I've been through a lot the last few months and anyone would feel that way with the weight of mountains on top of them."

"Owailion told me about your ...disagreement," she commented, trying to get it out in the air without going to even more painful subjects. A battle between magicians would never be a light ordeal but it was better than discussing Paget.

"Call it what it was: a slaughter. He always will win that battle and never have to touch a sword," Vamilion acknowledged.

"Why was he fighting you? It seemed silly, from what little Owailion told me," encouraged Gailin, showing that whatever it was that had ignited the feud, she would back Vamilion.

"It was silly," he confirmed. "I was frustrated... by many things, most of which had been exacerbated by Owailion. You see, I have no way of magically traveling. It's a limitation I cannot understand because all the other Wise Ones, Owailion, the Queen of Rivers...and now you, you all have a convenient and magical way to travel. That is why it was easier for Owailion to watch over you as you moved out onto the plains. Owailion was the one to suggest that, but he had ulterior motives apparently. He wanted me frustrated...angry even. He wanted me to worry about you out there alone with the snake."

"His name is Neeorm by the way," she said coldly, feeling the reptilian touch at her throat, and swallowed, wondering if Vamilion would interpret her comment as caring for her husband. "I wiped his mind and he's as much a patient here as my grandmother," she added to make it clear she did not love the man.

Vamilion nodded again, stiffly. He had not known what had become of his old enemy, but then he continued with a more present problem. "In reality Owailion was using us both. He wanted you driven into your powers and tapping into...Neeorm's mind to explore. We know very little about the magic of the Outlanders and you have discovered much Owailion values. He knew neither of us could get as close as you were already positioned. He also...and I cannot believe he could do this...he wanted you to marry the snake. He wanted," and Vamilion had to sigh deeply to get the next words out of his mouth before they made him ill. "He wanted to prove to me that Wise Ones cannot have children. You would not get pregnant. He thought that if I knew that my sons were not mine; that Paget had been unfaithful, then this was proof. He thought I would be angry enough to leave Paget and turn to you before she had passed."

Gailin felt her jaw drop in amazement. "He would let me...to force you...?"

Vamilion sighed in frustration. "Owailion always has many layers of plan. He also knew that I would then be angry enough to either follow you to kill Neeorm or...or do what I did. Crack open the Land and empty the ley lines."

"Did you truly do that?" Gailin asked, though she knew the answer. She had seen the evidence written in Drake's empty mind.

"Yes," Vamilion admitted with a touch of guilt. "I had to be so angry. I couldn't understand why Owailion had allowed you to...to be touched by that snake. I loved you too much already and Owailion refused to explain all this to me. I grew so angry with him, his manipulation, his devious mind...that I would rather fight him than all the invaders that are coming. I fought him and broke myself on something harder than a mountain. I will always lose to the King of Creating."

Gailin did not know what to say. Maybe there was nothing to say in this painful realization. He had fought his mentor, feared for Gailin's safety and sanity, broken the earth, fought an invasion and then discovered the woman he had loved had been unfaithful and his sons were not his. And on top of that, Paget had committed suicide? Vamilion must be going insane with grief, and yet he sat there speaking with her in even tones, steady and solid and strong. She marveled at the attraction he already held for her.

"And now I have to go tell my boys that their mother is dead," he announced grimly.

Gailin looked at him with sympathy. "How can I help?"

Vamilion glanced down in shame and yet still he was willing to ask anyway. "Will you take me to my sons? They live along the Laranian River and it would take me a month to walk there, but I should tell them in person. You don't have to meet them. That wouldn't be right, but..."

"Of course I will. While you talk to them, I can help with the healers in their village and they'll never know I was there. Do they know... about this compulsion... about what you and I will be?" she asked.

"I didn't tell them, but Paget might have. They haven't forgiven me for becoming a magician and that's bad enough. I won't tell them... what their mother did. Some things don't need to be known, even if they are the truth."

"When should we leave?" She drew her candle out to show him. "I think it's also able to work as your magic – mountain to mountain. If I give a candle to someone, they can call me without using magic and get my help. It's a perfect way for me to know where I am needed."

Vamilion looked worried, almost distressed at her comment. "It seems.....rather blatant. We've always tried to remain subtle with magic, so no one knows we are magicians and we have some anonymity."

But Gailin's Wise One instincts told her otherwise. She reached out and touched Vamilion's arm gently, waiting for him to look at her. Her green eyes calmed him and made him realize she carried with her an aura of peace neither Owailion nor he could match.

"My magic is different," she whispered. "I must be out and about, helping people. The healers in the villages have to know I exist and that they can call on me for help. It won't be enough for me to be compelled to investigate where I'm needed. I need to be known. It's time that the people of the Land stop things like that attempted hanging and set aside their general fear of magic. They must embrace the way it has developed here in the Land. Cutting off the ley lines will stop sorcerers like Drake from coming here again, and the people will be healed of their fear of magic."

Vamilion nodded as he recognized her logic. "You are truly a Wise One."

* * *

Two days later they stood side by side on the eastern banks of the Laranian River, just south of the village where Vamilion's sons had settled. They had buried Paget before they left, putting her to rest in a crypt that he cut magically in the side of the mountain above the palace. He had even carved a plaque into the stone face: Lady Paget of Vamilion, beloved wife and mother. He, Goren and Gailin were all that attended the memorial, and while it was brief, it resolved their sadness and Vamilion felt like he could move on, though where that would be, he did not know.

And he still did not know, beyond a small town on the Laranian River, how to find his sons. Once there he reached out his mind to locate their somewhat familiar thoughts and began walking, following his instincts to his eldest son's homestead out on the prairie. For her part Honiea marked a small village on the map she was finally enhancing with actual human habitation and then walked into the town to ask for the local healer. She could keep herself well occupied while Vamilion underwent that next uncomfortable conversation. She learned the name of the town and was just aiding the village healer with a better way to set broken limbs when she heard a voice in her head.

"It's time!" Owailion shouted, making her jump. "I need you both here immediately." The rude interruption could only be the King of Creating. She had almost forgotten that another invasion was coming and the Wise Ones would have to deal with it.

"I'm sorry," she told the village healer as she conjured a simple candle. That he did not react witnessed his comfort level with her gift of knowledge and magic. "I am being called elsewhere now. Remember, if you ever need my help, light this candle, hold it high and I will come as quickly as I can." She then hurriedly left the healer's clinic and stepped out onto the muddy road, fresh with spring rains. Debating about whether to go interrupt Vamilion, she reached out to his mind but before she could, he reached for her.

"Can you come to me here? Owailion's in a hurry and he'll be distressed if we aren't there instantly." Vamilion pressed an image of a bare oak tree in the farmyard of his son's home and himself standing beneath it. She used the candle to shift and found herself standing by his side.

Although he looked miserable, Vamilion smiled. "You are my Talisman. I will never have a magical way to go everywhere I need to go, but I will always have you. Thank you."

"How did it go with your son?" she asked carefully, feeling that Owailion could wait.

"He's upset, but surprisingly thankful I came. I told him nothing of how she died or that I am not his real father, but he almost forgave me. We might even eventually be friends I think…if I ever get a chance. Shall we go?"

"Owailion can wait," Honiea replied bluntly. "I need a visual if I am to go someplace. I've never gone that far without knowing whose mind through which I am seeing. Can you help me into wherever Owailion is?"

Vamilion nodded, closed his eyes in concentration, throwing his mind toward the east, groping for Owailion's presence and found him after a brief search on the east side of the Don River delta. "Look into my mind," Vamilion instructed and Honiea's tentative magic touched his soul, slipping easily into his brain and she had the visualization. She lit the candle with a thought, reached out to take Vamilion's hand

and then held the candle high, wishing to go where Owailion awaited them.

They arrived in a flash of lavender light on the flats with the thin forest before them and with the Don River behind them. A dark tower stood on the eastern shore beyond. It was short and ugly compared to the tall, graceful Wise One's palace in white marble that stood a few miles beyond out in the middle of the delta. That palace rose higher into the spring sky even though it was farther away. After turning to see where they had arrived, Vamilion smiled down at her, blew out the candle for her and then put his hand under her chin. "Like I said, my personal Talisman."

Gailin thrilled that he was opening up to her of his own self. He looked like he wanted to kiss her, but Owailion came striding out of the gate of the dark tower and trotted up to them, interrupting the moment and spoiling the mood. "I'm glad you two could make it. About time," Owailion commented.

Vamilion's eyes grew stormy, either because he didn't like the interference or he still had not forgiven his mentor for his manipulation. Either way, Honiea gave him a warning look to be sure he didn't lose his temper again and then turned toward Owailion with a winning smile and Vamilion had to do likewise.

He reluctantly turned to address Owailion. "May I introduce the Lady Honiea, Queen of Healing. The Lady Paget has died, but we came as soon as we heard you needed us."

That news brought Owailion up short. He had not known about Paget's death and now stumbled into the awkward silence. It took him a moment to recover and then he simply ignored the painful announcement altogether.

"Welcome, Lady Honiea. I'm glad you're here. We are going to need all our efforts on this attack. It will take all three of us." He then launched into the circumstances that had decided him on calling them. "The Outlanders have been coming by land up through the Demion forest and will be here any day. I've built these towers to keep watch, but now they are reaching the edge of where Vamilion has broken the ley lines. They will soon discover the end of their power. Honiea, this is also where we discover if your dark magician husband has shared your true name with them. If he was in contact with these Outlanders, then they might come beyond their connection to the ley lines in order to go after you. They'll be vulnerable. However, if they do not know of your name, or even of your existence, we want to show them that the Land has yet another defender and convince them that the Land might as well be sealed again to them."

"So you mean for them to see her?" Vamilion's voice grew thunderous. "You want to test out the theory of whether they know her name by letting them witness her here and try name magic again. That's the most ridiculous thing I've heard from you yet. You'll put her out there as a fuse to explode the situation. I've noticed that whether the gems are in the mine or not, it never works out so well for the ones caught in that explosion." Vamilion advanced on Owailion with a murderous look in his eyes.

"No," Honiea objected, stepping between the two men and deliberately put her hand on Vamilion's chest, directly over his heart. "No, Wise Ones must not fight."

Vamilion looked down at her in wonder. How could she be so forgiving when Owailion had thrown her to the wolves?

"I can overlook the past because I cannot heal your rift if I hold a grudge. I have cleansed that past. There is something safer we can do instead of daring these dark sorcerers to come away from their ley lines."

Honiea didn't lower her hand, but instead stood her ground between the two men and explained the plan that had come full blown into her mind. In a way it seemed fitting that it came down to her to heal their rift and stitch up the gaping wounds that had afflicted the Land since the day the Seal had been broken. And her plan hopefully would do both.

"When I traveled with Drake, I noticed he discounted all my healing magic, but truly coveted other things about Wise One power that seemed to impress him far more. He marveled at the palaces: we passed by three of them before we found mine. He railed at the seals around them and grumbled at the waste of magical energy needed to maintain what he thought were silly protections. He had to preserve his power like precious water. And the royal clothing; he could not figure out how we had the magical stamina to do that change but he found it most impressive. If we made such a display, blatant and excessive, it makes an impact on these sorcerers. If I conjured a diamond he valued it more than a rabbit in our dinner pot."

"And he had no idea that diamonds are easier?" Owailion commented. "Interesting. So what kind of flashy display would convince them that they are not welcome and never will be?"

Chapter 18

The Wall

The forest bristled with power lurking in the dark as hundreds of Outlander sorcerers approached. In the tower named Right, the few armed men Owailion had gathered to defend the place looked intimidating in the armor that the Wise Ones had given them, polished and strong. They guarded over Honiea and her prisoner, thinking they were there to protect her. They had no idea she would be defending them. Even through the thick granite walls of the Right Tower, she could sense the sorcerers that had gathered to invade the Land. They had reached not twenty miles away, still in the forest but now they knew their ley lines had gone missing. The line they had followed had petered out.

Meanwhile Owailion stood a few miles east of the tower, concentrating on magic farther afield. He and Vamilion were enacting Honiea's plan. They stood five hundred miles apart, but working together, toward each other, creating a wall of resistance beyond anything man made before. Honiea's understanding of the dark sorcerers like Drake had convinced them that only such a grand gesture would repel this type of attack forever. Indeed they had bet their entire strategy on the prospect. Between the two of them, Vamilion and Owailion had spent three days building a Wall to define the border of the Land.

Five hundred miles away, at the southern end of the Great Chain on top of the new peak he had built in the midst of his battle with Owailion, Vamilion had set up his work place. Below him he saw the slowly dying Demion forest spreading out, but his mind was even farther away. He cast his magic far to the northwest of the Land, beyond Jonjonel, to a plain of empty land, completely devoid of people and few animals on the tundra. There awaited stone. He need not make this Wall from nothing. This stone, ancient, compressed granite and useless for any other purpose would be his raw material. With his talent with rock he magically rough cut eight by eight blocks of the stuff and then magically transported them across the continent with a thought to him at his work site on the mountain. There he refined his cuts and then transitioned each cut stone over to Owailion who shifted them into the trough he had cut through the forest. Over and over again they did this, carving stones that a man would take days with a saw to cut free. Together they did this twenty times in an hour, building the wall deep and tall. Then Honiea finally sealed it all in a magical repellent she crafted over every inch of the stone as each was placed.

And so, over the next three days, as the sorcerers approached, the Wall slowly emerged, from the base of the Right Tower toward the mountains where Vamilion stood to oversee his creation. Together they worked almost constantly, crafting it too high to climb easily, higher than the trees around it and the gray, polished surface loomed out of nowhere, cutting across well-traveled roads, blocking creeks that normally would feed into the Don. With Vamilion's affinity for stone and Owailion's expertise for engineering they were able to craft three miles of barrier in a day, deliberately building right in front of the incoming invaders. While it would not block them physically for long, the intimidation of encountering such an obstacle in the middle of the forest where none was before, might make them hesitate. The Wise Ones needed that hesitation, or they would end up in a pitched magical battle; three against hundreds. They needed to give these Outlanders a reason to leave.

Finally, when the Wall stretched beyond the Right to the horizon Honiea went to retrieve Vamilion and bring him back to his handiwork for the final confrontation. He was exhausted after the long hauling of stones from three thousand miles away, but that couldn't be helped. He was the only one who could sense the ley lines just beyond the Wall and the next phase of their plan demanded that skill. They had built as much of the barrier as they could before the sorcerers arrived but now they must stop building and prepare for the standoff.

All three of the Wise Ones climbed on top of the Wall as the sun began to rise. With the dawn light in their eyes, and the first warm day of the season facing them, they stood ready to challenge the Outlanders who had come. All the preparations set and from the safety of a sealed and magically defended obstacle, the Wise Ones made a stoic defense.

And hundreds of Outlanders gathered at the base of the Wall. Honiea could sense them; on horses, in grand carriages, and even a few moving about as something other than human. The lure of the Land, with its open territory and almost limitless, untapped potential made them covet the place of which many may had only heard. Drake must have told them something, for they came directly up a strong ley line Vamilion had marked on his map that ran right under the Vamilion Mountains and out into the forest. It must have lured them in and now they found it cut off. So they didn't know that Vamilion had broken off all the ley lines on the west side of the Wall.

Owailion stood atop the Wall in his royal regalia, white leather studded with diamonds and gold inlay. In his hand he held a platinum sword and in the other, a globe of crystal. What this globe accomplished, Honiea could only guess, but she hoped to discover more soon. For her own part, she had returned to the lovely embroidered lavender gown. This time she also wore a corset of silver steel, adorned with lilies and at her back she boasted a crystal quiver full of arrows she didn't know how to use and in her hand, a silver bow. Vamilion's appearance complemented hers, with armor etched with mountain scenes and in one hand a stone hammer while in the other, he held a sword that boasted a blood-red pommel. They must have made an impressive display to the Outlanders who looked up at them.

Owailion peered down over the forest and saw the dumbfounded eyes of the Outlanders and smiled. "Stop," he said in the language of the Land, speaking softly and letting magic amplify his voice toward the ground where it rippled through the gathering. "You may come no farther."

Honiea could hear them chattering in confusion or wonder. Perhaps they did not understand his language but Vamilion did and shared privately what words echoed up to them atop the Wall. "They are bewildered, for they did not know that we knew they were coming. They are amazed by the Wall and wonder where the power to build it is coming from. Perhaps it is an illusion, they guess."

"Then show them," Honiea suggested.

Vamilion, the only one of the three who could sense the ley lines, took the frayed edge of the line east of the Wall and directed its energy right into the structure they had built, reinforcing it beyond even their own power to do so. The magic in the ley line began flowing into the stone and the Wall soaked it up, draining it as fast as the river of magic filled. Vamilion even used the ley line to continue the illusion of more Wall even though it had not been built as yet. The appearance of stone spread and pushed into the sea and up into the Great Chain, completing the border of the Land. It said emphatically that no one may pass this border without permission and magic would defend the line.

As the ley line's power became unavailable some of the sorcerers began to faint, wavering in their power as the Wall sucked their lifeblood from them. Honiea saw this as a signal and brought forth her prisoner. She broke the invisibility spell she maintained over Drake and he staggered forward so those below could see.

Then she raised her voice to be heard by them. "This is what will happen to any sorcerer who enters the Land from now on. There are no ley lines west of here any longer and this one you followed now feeds the barrier of this Wall. Do you wish to become a witless baby like Drake? If so, challenge us and suffer as he has."

"You have no power for this!" someone shouted up toward the three Wise Ones, using magic to be heard. "You could not break the ley lines. A sorcerer such as Drake could not be overcome. This is an illusion and we will see how long your magic Wall can last."

So Owailion revealed their next step. He allowed the guards they had prepared to appear. These soldiers, in front of the entire assembly, carefully tied a rope around Drake's neck with the knot at the back of his head. Then Honiea whispered in Drake's ear. "Neeorm, sit on the edge of the Wall." Drake did as ordered, not even focusing out over the forest or to where his compatriots awaited him while the soldiers held his leash carefully. Then Honiea whispered once again, "Neeorm, go over the edge of the Wall."

Drake obeyed. He began to strangle as he fell, but the soldiers lowered him ever so slowly so he would not break his neck. The horrified Outlanders began shouting out spells, trying to cut the rope, or blast pure waves of power at the Wall to break the enchantments on it. Nothing touched Drake, the Wall or anyone atop the structure. Owailion's crystal globe projected a shimmering glass-like shield over the affected area, pushing away even the few trees that had survived the Wall's excavation. Then when Drakes body had reached half way down the side of the Wall the soldiers stopped lowering their victim. He was out of range to rescue physically but fully on display against the side of the Wall. On instinct, the witless sorcerer kicked and strangled, beating his heels against the stone but he never uttered even a moan of pain. As the blasts of power hit at the Wall, he didn't possess the wits cry out in alarm.

Someone below in the forest must have known Drake's true name, for he shouted up to the struggling body. "Neeorm, break the rope." Nothing happened though as he continued to thrash and struggle for every breath. Drake did not have the magic or physical ability to break through his noose and though he tried to obey, it was hopeless.

"Have we made ourselves clear? There will be no magic in the Land but Wise One magic. You are not welcome here. We protect the people and will cut off any who mean this Land harm," Honiea announced down into the forest for all to hear. "I have complete control of him and all the ley lines have been shattered. You will gain nothing here. Go back to your homes and leave the Land in peace."

The blasts and curses continued to flow up from the forest and smashed against the Wall that did not even tremble. Then Vamilion raised his hands and the earthquakes began. The startled horses bolted and great cracks in the earth swallowed those unable to escape magically. The Outlander's power thrown against the Wall flickered as even that last ley line dried up and slid into the earth to become part of the well magic. Then finally Owailion invoked his crystal globe again. A wave of blue light pushed out from the orb he held, brushing away everything it encountered. Trees snapped and men were washed away like a tsunami swept them ahead of the force. He continued to expand it until all nine miles of the wall was protected under his shield and the Outlanders could no longer be seen. The forest, turned into splinters, began to glow with a blue fire and erupted with pent up magic that pushed eastward into Demion, burning away the shelter of anyone who hoped to approach the Wall. No one came back to challenge them. The Outlanders fled, having endured long enough with weak ley lines and the strange magic of the Land.

Accordingly Owailion pulled his blue shield back into the globe and motioned for the men to pull the husk of Drake back up onto the top of the Wall. He was dead; strangled, or weakened beyond breathing, no one could tell. With a sigh Owailion instructed the soldiers to return to Right and bury the corpse.

Meanwhile Vamilion sat down with his legs over the lip of the Wall and looked out over the devastation they had caused and wondered if they dare relax. Would the intimidation of Wise One power be enough to keep the Outlanders away, or would a true face to face battle still be required? He must have been sharing that thought absently, for Honiea came to him and sat down as well.

"Probably not forever, but for now," she commented simply.

Vamilion sighed. "I was wrong."

"About what?" she asked as she watched Owailion magically lowering the soldiers down the western side, off the Wall, returning them to Right where there would probably be a permanent garrison now that they had a physical border to defend.

"Many things, but most especially about you. You are more than a Talisman for me. You are an exquisite jewel. I would not have thought of this kind of display. Neither would Owailion. We need you to keep us from going mad. There is a reason Wise Ones come in pairs. We might not require a mate but we are far better a person when we have that other with us. I was also wrong to not have sought you earlier. I should have protected you as well as kept my oath to Paget. There must have been a better way. It would have prevented much of the foolish fighting Owailion and I have done and so much that was...wrong, would not have happened to you. I'm sorry you had to endure the Soul Eater."

"Is this true, what I hear?" Owailion mocked from several feet away. "Is Vamilion actually admitting he should have followed my advice far earlier and gone Seeking for his mate?" His sarcasm felt less than playful given his normal sour attitude, but from Owailion this came as practically a joke.

"I was admitting that to her, not to you. I'll take her advice over yours every time," Vamilion commented in a reluctant humility. Then quite deliberately he reached for Honiea's hand, taking it in his, holding it and tracing the lines in her palm, as if memorizing them. He felt fascination for the shape and gentle touch she could manage with these healing hands. Then he continued as if Owailion hadn't interrupted. "And I suppose that means I have to ask you if you will wait for me to finish building this Wall before we do much more...in a relationship. It might take time for me to be ready. Will you wait?"

Honiea sighed, thinking about all the mending there remained to do. She wanted to go meet every village healer and share candles with them. She needed to go speak with the Apothecary and finally introduce herself to him. Another Talisman awaited her to find as well before she could finally break the seal on her palace, though she doubted she would spend much time there, given her gifts. She technically was no longer married, since Drake had died, so she was free now, but of course she would wait for Vamilion to overcome his grief for Paget. She felt not a drop of loss for Drake's demise. She could occupy herself for as long as it took and looked forward with anticipation. With an eternal life and calling, she could afford to be patient.

However, for one thing she did not have to wait. Tentatively Vamilion reached out and hesitatingly lifted her chin so he could see her deep green eyes. "May I kiss you?" he asked shyly, like he had never done this before. In a strange way he had not and neither had she. To both of them, that kiss was the first of an eternity.

Epilogue

He hiked up the mountainside rather than going instantly. He had to think about things before he attempted this. Somehow it was important that he tell someone, anyone, about what he was going to do. And if the only other person in the world to care wasn't a human....well, he had to try. He had four years until the volcano erupted again and if he didn't do this now, he might never get a chance again. And so, Owailion walked slowly up the slopes of Jonjonel, his birthplace, at least in the Land.

At the top he looked back over the terrain and was once again impressed. The Land was a beautiful place and always had been. To the west he saw the ocean, blue and reflecting back the sun at him. To the south he saw the green blanket of the Fallon Forest stretching beyond the horizon. To the east he saw the beginnings of the Great Chain Mountains where the new Queen would soon be setting up her home. And to the north the tundra spread for miles in a frosting of lavender, pink, white and yellow flowers that would remain only for a few weeks during this, the height of summer. He had hoped to see much of this untouched, but now it was open to invasion and he must protect the Land.

He must protect it from Owailion himself as well. He felt miserable with what he had done. Vamilion and Honiea were right in accusing him of manipulating them and their magic for his own ends. Did the ends justify the means? He wanted to protect the Land and reseal it from the Outlanders that invaded. Wasn't that a worthy goal? He had thought so, but when his efforts to crack the ley lines and beat back the invaders allowed Honiea to be enslaved and had forced Vamilion to break his oaths and his back, well that went too far and Owailion now acknowledged it. He had become a danger to the Land.

But he still had goals. He could not stop all the invaders. He had to admit that most of the immigration into this empty Land had come as a benefit. He would never get sixteen Wise Ones and reseal the Land if he never let someone in.

The doors were open now. Vamilion and Honiea would teach and invite new Wise Ones. They needed no help from him, especially if his aid was toxic and manipulative. It would be better if he stayed out of the way, in his own palace and let the world rest from his efforts. But part of him still wanted the approval from a higher authority of his decision to become a hermit. He could pray about it but his prayers remained unanswered, at least in the obvious manner.

So he came here to Jonjonel for the next best thing. With his mind Owailion reached out into the sky from this tallest spot in the Land, seeking the mind of his mentor, hoping Mohan would still waken and talk him out of some foolishness before he committed himself to a life without human interaction.

"Mohan, are you awake?" Owailion asked desperately and apologetic, like a little boy afraid of the dark. "I want to tell you something. I've done something terrible. I've hurt the only friends I have and they might not forgive me. Are you there, old friend?"

He heard no reply from anyone; not the dragon, if he was even out there, or God, who Owailion knew was always there, even if He did not make Himself known. Instead Owailion looked up to see clouds gathering, thick and stormy, even in the otherwise clear weather. He knew what this meant and fell down onto his knees and looked down, not wanting to even see the storm that meant his chastisement approached.

"My son, you are so torn. Where did you set your hope? Did you give up?" the voice from his dreams echoed in his head once again. "Why?"

Owailion sighed. "There is no excuse for losing hope except that I lost Raimi too. I need her like I need magic to stay alive. How can I go on? I hurt everyone around me when I try to find a way to bring her back, making it worse."

"You are like a stone, standing alone, worn away before its time. When you stand alone, you protect nothing, build nothing and are worth nothing. The other Wise Ones as they come will each protect you and give you a key to finding what you have lost. Do not shut them out. Be patient. You must not give up hope or you will lose the chance to retrieve your companion. Every Wise One to come will have something to help you or remind you of what you are pursuing. Have hope, Owailion, and she will come."

Owailion looked up at the glowing storm clouds. Could he believe this message? Always, despite the presence of clouds, he felt nothing but love from God. However, Owailion had lost so much he had let his cynicism block out God's voice. But Owailion clung to that promised hope. With all the power at his disposal and all the time in the world, he still needed to be reassured that he could do this.

A second voice abruptly impinged on his awareness, deep, grumbling and half asleep. "*Yes, and now be good and go say you're sorry.*" Then Mohan went back to his interrupted nap.

Dear reader,

We hope you enjoyed reading *Ley Lines*. Please take a moment to leave a review, even if it's a short one. Your opinion is important to us.

Discover more books by Lisa Lowell at
https://www.nextchapter.pub/authors/lisa-lowell

Want to know when one of our books is free or discounted? Join the newsletter at
http://eepurl.com/bqqB3H

Best regards,
Lisa Lowell and the Next Chapter Team

The story continues in:

Life Giver by Lisa Lowell

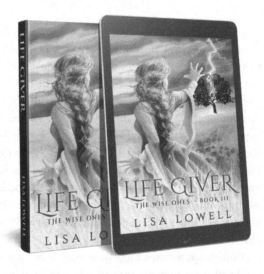

To read the first chapter for free, please head to:
https://www.nextchapter.pub/books/life-giver

About the Author

Lisa Lowell was born in 1967 into a large family full of hands-on artists, in southern Oregon. In an effort to avoid conflict, her art of choice was always writing, something both grandmothers taught her. She started with poetry at six on her grandmother's ancient manual typewriter. By her teens she moved on to pen and paper and produced gloomy, angst-ridden fantasy during adolescence. Her mother claims that Lisa shut the door and never came out until she left for university. During this time she felt compelled to draw illustrations throughout the margins that helped supplement her neglect of adjectives and consistent story lines.

A much appreciated English teacher, Mrs. Segetti, collected these moody musings and sent them in to scholarship foundations. Lisa got a scholarship for that rather poor writing, escaped Oregon and went to university. While she loved her family, her only requirement in a school was anywhere too far away to come home on weekends. She got as far as Idaho, Utah and then even Washington D.C. before she truly launched. She traveled to Sweden (Göteborg, Lund and Sundsvall) for a year and a half during college where she also reconnected with her heritage.

During college Lisa also fell in love and then had her heart broken. Suddenly she had something to write about. Every story written since harbors a romance and a tangled journey; a saga as it were, where the tale comes back to the start. She started to tap into Scandinavian myth and overcame fears of writing conflict. All her earlier failed starts and fascinating characters now molded into an actual story. Completing her degrees in Secondary Education and Masters in English as a Second Language at Western Oregon University, Lisa continued to travel and read favorite authors; Lloyd Alexander, David Brin, Patricia McKillip and Anne McCaffrey. She graduated with a teaching degree 1993.

Then, when she came back to Oregon, like a fairy tale, she met Pat Lowell. They met on Sunday, played racquet ball on Monday night and were engaged by the end of the date. The sense of peace in meeting someone with the same goals and values made it right. Four months later they were married. Lisa began reworking childhood manuscripts into credible stories, and this was when Sea Queen began. When children did not arrive as expected, the Lowells adopted three children, Travis, Scott and Kiana. At that point, Lisa chose to ease off writing actively for a time to focus on her family. However, she kept all the ideas and honed her skill while teaching Middle School English. Storytelling remained her true talent and made her a skillful teacher. In 2011 she was named VFW Oregon Teacher of the Year.

In 2012 a friend asked for manuscripts so he could learn how to get a book onto Amazon in e-book form. As she had several half finished works she could contribute, Lisa gave him one and when she saw how easy that seemed, the idea of publishing snuck up on her again. Her children were moving on, and she felt she could again begin to write. She reworked the first book in the Wise Ones series, Sea Queen, and began sharing it with beta readers. However, her friends wanted to hear the back-stories of some of the other characters so she started writing those into full manuscripts and realized that a series was born.

Publishing became more important when Pat had a terrible accident and developed Parkinsons. Lisa had to stay closer to home to help him and he encouraged her writing. She continued to teach English in middle school (someone has to) and blogs on a Facebook page at https://www.facebook.com/vikingauthor/ . At present she is developing a Word Press for her future work and tinkering with her next novels, Markpath, a set of sci-fi novels. She loves to write but also experiments with drawing, dances while she writes, sings when the radio is on and reads a great deal of poorly written essays by thirteen year olds. She still lives in Oregon, near waterfalls and Powells, the best bookstore on earth. She is still in love with her husband Pat and still loves writing tangled journeys.

The Wise Ones

Book 1 - Talismans
Book 2 - Ley Lines

Ley Lines
ISBN: 978-4-86751-578-5 (Mass Market)

Published by
Next Chapter
1-60-20 Minami-Otsuka
170-0005 Toshima-Ku, Tokyo
+818035793528
5th July 2021

CPSIA information can be obtained
at www.ICGtesting.com
Printed in the USA
LVHW030537270721
693792LV00006B/522